Jake said to Susannah, leaning across the passenger seat.

Several of the women at the bus stop looked at Susannah in astonishment.

"Why, uh…thank you, Mr. Taggart. It's kind of you to offer a ride, but there's no need. The bus will be here any second," she said in an ultrapolite voice, begging him with her eyes not to do this.

Jake ignored her silent plea. "Get in, Susannah," he insisted. "Or I'll get out and put you in. Which will it be?"

The wide-eyed gazes of their audience swept between them. Left with no choice, Susannah hurriedly slipped into the car.

For a moment they just sat there and Susannah was terrified that he might kiss her in front of everybody.

"Why did you do that?"

"Do what?"

"Why did you pick me up? Now everyone will think we're involved."

"Susannah, we *are* involved."

Dear Reader,

Thanksgiving is the one holiday in the year where the whole family gathers for that traditional turkey dinner with all the trimmings. And who can resist just one extra helping of stuffing or pumpkin pie!

Silhouette Romance novels make perfect Thanksgiving reading. They're a celebration of family and all the traditional values we hold so dear. *And* they're about the perfect love that leads to marriage and happy-ever-afters.

This month we're featuring one of our best-loved authors, Brittany Young—not to mention the ever-popular Arlene James and Marcine Smith, and the talented Pat Tracy and Patti Standard. And to round out the month we're continuing our WRITTEN IN THE STARS series with the passionate Scorpio hero in Ginna Gray's *Sting of the Scorpion*. What a lineup! And in months to come, watch for Diana Palmer, Annette Broadrick and *all* your favorites!

The authors and editors of Silhouette Romance books strive to bring you the best in romance fiction, stories that capture the laughter, the tears—the sheer joy—of falling in love. Let us know if we've succeeded. We'd love to hear from you!

Happy Reading,

Valerie Susan Hayward
Senior Editor

GINNA GRAY

Sting of
the Scorpion

Silhouette *Romance*
Published by Silhouette Books New York
America's Publisher of Contemporary Romance

SILHOUETTE BOOKS
300 E. 42nd St., New York, N.Y. 10017

STING OF THE SCORPION

ISBN: 0-373-08826-4

First Silhouette Books printing November 1991

Printed in the U.S.A.

GINNA GRAY

A native Houstonian, Ginna Gray admits that, since childhood, she has been a compulsive reader as well as a head-in-the-clouds dreamer. Long accustomed to expressing her creativity in tangible ways (Ginna also enjoys painting and needlework), she finally decided to try putting her fantasies and wild imaginings down on paper. The result? The mother of two now spends eight hours a day as a full-time writer.

A Note From The Author:

Dear Reader,

Do you like your heroes tall, dark and dangerous?
How about intense, secretive and determined?
Brooding? Passionate? All of the above?

If the answer is yes, then get ready to fall in love.

I did—and that was during the research stage, before
I even wrote *Sting of the Scorpion*.

In digging through countless books on astrology, I
became fascinated by these powerful, sensual,
enigmatic alpha males. I mean, whew! Who could
resist a man who is cool and calm on the outside and
a seething caldron of red-hot passion on the inside?
A man who can be tough as nails when he has to be,
then tap into that deep, inscrutable nature and treat a
woman with an exquisite tenderness that will make
her melt and run right down into her shoes. Not me.
And I sincerely hope, dear reader, not you.

They say that a Scorpio has a mystical, hypnotic
appeal that is irresistible to women, so why fight it?
Just sit back, kick off your shoes and enjoy.

Happy reading,

Ginna Gray

Chapter One

Jake Taggart missed little. Still, if it hadn't been for her hair, he might not have noticed her right away.

Fresh back from Germany and intensive, week-long negotiations with the Weissman execs, Jake's mind was occupied with facts and figures and stratagem as he stepped from the elevator on the executive floor of Jetco's corporate headquarters. He was halfway across the outer office when a movement happened to draw his attention.

His sideways glance was merely reflex, but when his gaze encountered the glorious mane of silver-blond hair, he did a double-take and stared, his steps faltering.

Jake's heart slammed against his ribs. His jaw tightened and his eyes narrowed. In his thirty-six years he had seen hair that color in only one family. They all had it. Every one of them. Even Seth.

Around him, the large outer office hummed with sounds of activity—the click of computer keyboards, the electronic chirp of telephones, the murmur of voices, the almost inaudible whir of laser printers and fax machines.

Jake stood still. His gaze bore into the woman's downbent head. Silently he willed her to look up from the stack of charts she was earnestly studying.

"Is there something I can do for you, Mr. Taggart?"

The diffident question intruded, bringing awareness of his surroundings and the curious glances he was attracting from his employees. Jake's stare switched to Thelma Stoddard, the supervisor of the typing pool. Her thin mouth twitched in an ingratiating smile, her pale eyes both anxious and inquisitive behind the steel-rimmed glasses perched on the end of her nose.

"No, nothing," he snapped, and strode away, down the hallway that held the executive offices, the talk he had intended to have with Grant Calloway, Jetco's top vice president, forgotten.

"Alice, come in here." Jake marched through his administrative assistant's office and into his own without slowing or giving her a chance to respond.

When seated behind his desk, he watched Alice's unhurried progress. Not one whit ruffled by his peremptory manner and narrow-eyed stare, she sauntered across the plush carpet with all the panache and elegant grace of a runway model. Eyeing him wryly, she lowered her slender frame into the chair before the desk and smoothed the skirt of her tangerine-and-beige suit. When done, she ran her hand over her perfectly coiffed gray hair and cocked one eyebrow. "And good morning to you, too, Jacob," she said with a dry smile.

With the exception of Grant, Alice was the only person who was not intimidated by Jake. She had been with him for nine years—ever since he'd started the J. E. Taggart Company, otherwise known as Jetco—far too long to be in awe of him.

Not that Alice ever had been. She was much too sensible and self-assured to be bowled over by anyone. The trait was one of the things Jake admired and valued most about her.

Usually her sarcasm amused him, but not today.

He gave her a hard look and tipped his head toward the outer office. "Who's the blonde?"

"My new assistant. You told me to hire someone. Remember?"

"What's she doing out there?"

"Learning the office. With you out of town, I figured this was the best time for her to familiarize herself with how things work around here. She's spent a day in each of the departments. Why? Is there a problem?"

"No, no problem." Jake tapped the eraser end of a pencil against the surface of the mahogany desk. He watched the bouncing action, his face carefully inscrutable. "What's her name?"

"Dushay. Susannah Dushay."

The name went through Jake like a hot dagger and caused his entire body to quicken. He'd known it! From the instant he'd set eyes on her he'd known.

Jake's heart pounded. He had to struggle to hide the excitement he felt. He forced himself to breathe slowly and evenly, despite the constriction in his chest. Propping his elbows on the padded arms of his chair, he steepled his fingers and looked at Alice over them. "Send her in. If she's going to be working closely with me, we'd better get acquainted."

"Now?" Alice glanced at the briefcase lying on the corner of his desk, then at her boss. Her hazel eyes narrowed. "What's your hurry? I thought you'd be anxious to brief Grant and me on the details of the Weissman deal and hear how his California trip went. He just got in a few minutes ago, himself."

"Later." Jake's low voice and steady look carried a subtle warning.

No fool, Alice knew when to back off. She rose and left the office without another word.

Five minutes later Alice ushered her new assistant into Jake's office, and his heart gave another jerk when he found himself looking into eyes the color of spring leaves.

Oh, yes, he thought, she was most definitely a Dushay. The family had a distinctive look about them—a combination of silver-gilt hair, fine-boned aristocratic features, green eyes and a slender build that gave them a refined appearance and set them apart from ordinary mortals.

Growing up as he had in the small east Texas town of Zach's Corners, Texas, Jake had learned early to recognize the breed.

His body thrummed and his pulse rate speeded up, but his remote expression stayed in place. With deceptive outer calm, he finished scribbling a note on a lined yellow pad before rising.

As Alice made the introduction, Jake murmured the appropriate words and politely shook Susannah Dushay's hand across the top of the desk. The feel of her soft palm trembling against his sent a jolt of electricity up his arm. He gritted his teeth, not liking the sensation, but the flash of alarm in her eyes told him she had felt it, as well, and her dismay gave him an odd sense of satisfaction.

"Won't you have a seat, Miss Dushay," he said, indicating the chairs grouped before his desk. "Alice, hold my calls for the next half hour." The order was a clear dismissal, one that drew an arch look from his assistant, but Jake's eyes never left Susannah.

He was struck by two things as he watched her ease into one of the straight-backed chairs and clasp her hands together in her lap. First, she was younger than he had expected. Second, she appeared nervous.

That she was beautiful came as no surprise at all. He would have been shocked had she not been, since striking good looks ran in the Dushay family.

Neither was her reaction an unusual one. Jake knew that many people found his intensity disturbing. At times he even used the discomfort of others to his advantage. That he had managed to unnerve one of the high and mighty Dushays, however, both surprised and pleased him.

His eyes flickered over her anxious face and stiff posture. "Relax. This is not an inquisition. I merely thought that, since we will be working together, you and I should meet."

He watched her, waiting for her to admit that they had already met, or at least that she knew who he was, but a fluttery smile was her only reply. Leaning back in his chair, Jake braced his elbows on the arms, laced his fingers together across his lean middle and pinned her with a probing look.

"Tell me, Miss Dushay. Why are you here?"

A dart of alarm ran through Susannah at the unexpected question. Surely she hadn't heard him right. "S-sir?"

"What do you expect to gain?"

His questions didn't make any sense. Oh, Lord. Had she missed something? She was so nervous it was certainly possible. All week, she'd been dreading this interview. "I . . . I'm afraid I don't understand."

Jake Taggart's gaze bore into her. He didn't move. He didn't even blink. He simply studied her with that intense stare of his. Susannah experienced an overwhelming urge to squirm, and she shifted uneasily before she caught herself. Now she knew how an insect felt under a high-powered microscope. Those penetrating gray eyes seemed to look right into her soul.

"This job? How do you see it?" Jake asked finally. "Are you merely looking for something to occupy your time?"

The question was almost funny, given her circumstances, but before Susannah could reply, Jake went on in the same mildly curious tone.

"Or are you perhaps planning to build a career? Maybe you have hopes of taking over Alice's job completely someday soon. Using it as a stepping stone to bigger and better things." The corners of Jake's mouth twitched, just a hint of a smile that did not reach his eyes or alter their piercing stare. "If that's the case, I'm afraid you're in for a disappointment. Alice may be pushing sixty, but there's a lot of life in the old gal yet. She won't retire, and I won't force her to. When she leaves this place, we'll have to carry her out, feet first."

Susannah blinked at him, alarm beginning to mingle with the confusion and nervousness she already felt. "M-Mr. Taggart...sir...I—I'm not after her job. Honestly."

The idea was ludicrous. Heavens! She felt extremely lucky to have landed the job as Alice's assistant. It was much more than she had dared to hope for, given her limited experience.

Why on earth was he asking her these bizarre questions?

It struck Susannah that possibly she had angered him in some way. Or worse, maybe he simply disliked her. The very idea brought a rush of panic.

No. No, of course not. You're just being foolish, she assured herself hastily. They had only just met. How could he dislike her? She'd probably just imagined that trace of anger in his voice.

Susannah swallowed hard. Perhaps. But there was no mistaking the coldness in his eyes. They were like shreds of ice...and just as piercing.

Jake fell silent again, and Susannah gripped her hands tighter together. His method of interviewing was shredding her nerves, which had been frayed to begin with. Between the startling questions and long silences, she was ready to scream. And did he have to keep looking at her like that?

"I see," Jake murmured thoughtfully after an interminable time. "Then tell me. Why *did* you seek employment here?"

"Why, to—"

The intercom buzzer cut her off before she could finish.

Jake pressed the talk button and snapped, "I said no calls."

"I know," came Alice's unruffled voice. "But Mr. Weissman is on the line from Germany. I figured you would want to speak to him."

"Right. Put him through."

Seeing her chance, Susannah grabbed at it. "I'll just get out of your way," she murmured, but when she started to rise, Jake waved her back down and cupped his hand over the mouthpiece.

"Sit tight. This won't take but a minute."

With a wan smile and a sinking sensation in the pit of her stomach, Susannah subsided into the chair. As Jake talked to Mr. Weissman she sat rigid, her nerves jangling. She couldn't botch this interview. She simply couldn't. This job was too important to her. She couldn't lose it now.

Oh, but she could, she reminded herself despondently. And it would serve her right for counting her chickens before they hatched. Alice had made it clear when she hired her that she had the job subject to Jake Taggart's approval.

And if the vibrations Susannah was picking up were anything to go by, she was as good as gone.

She should have taken the proviso more to heart and not gotten her hopes up. But, heaven help her, she hadn't been able to curb her elation. She needed this job so desperately. This past week she'd been so foolishly happy, sure that her problems were over.

What an optimistic fool she'd been. She should have known the job was too good to be true.

Actually, she hadn't really expected to get it. Of the women the employment agency had sent over, she had been the least qualified. She almost hadn't bothered to apply, but the excellent salary had been too tempting. At first, she hadn't believed her luck when Alice had taken a liking to her.

All week, though, underneath her happiness, she'd been dreading this interview. She'd had too little experience dealing with people to be comfortable in this sort of pressure situation. Certainly nothing in her life so far had prepared her for someone as intense and dynamic as Jake Taggart.

Chewing on her inner lip, Susannah peeked at Jake. All week she had been hearing about him from the other Jetco employees. Men and women alike spoke of him with a respectful deference that bordered on awe. From what she'd gleaned, Jake Taggart was intense, tough, bold and as cool as they came, a brilliant businessman who, in nine short years, had built his company from a shoestring operation, manufacturing computer components out of a rented warehouse, into a multimillion dollar, multifaceted worldwide concern.

"Jake's got the brains of a Harvard Business School grad and the brass and savvy of a street tough," his Gulf Coast District Manager had told her when she had been working in his department. There had been pride and respect in the man's voice, along with a touch of envy.

In connection with her new boss, over and over Susannah had heard words like drive and confidence and power. After meeting him, she didn't doubt it for a second.

Pretending disinterest, Susannah lowered her gaze to her folded hands and studied Jake through the screen of her lashes.

He said little. With his chair turned away from his desk, he held the receiver to his ear and stared out the glass outer wall. Now and then he inserted an incisive comment into the conversation, but mostly he listened, his narrowed eyes fixed on a distant point. His emotions, if he had any, were well hidden behind an inscrutable expression. Even his body language gave little away.

Still, Susannah sensed a boiling inner nature. Except for his free hand, which absently toyed with the coiled telephone cord, Jake sat immobile, but beneath that outward calm the man fairly crackled with electric vitality.

Susannah felt it radiating from him, reaching out and touching her across the few feet separating them. Gooseflesh rippled over her skin. She shivered and rubbed her forearms.

The slow movements of his hand drew Susannah's gaze. She watched him wind the coiled cord around his forefinger, then unwind it and wind it again, over and over. The repetitive action was slow and somehow sensual. Hypnotic.

His hand was large and utterly masculine, the palm broad, the fingers long and blunt. Susannah got a funny feeling in her stomach. She had never noticed before how beautiful a man's hands could be.

A starched white cuff extended a half inch from the arm of his gray suit coat, in sharp contrast to his dark skin and the crisp black hair sprinkled over the back of his hand. Gold winked from beneath the cuff, and she caught a glimpse of a wafer-thin watch.

Mesmerized, Susannah let her gaze drift upward. The impeccably tailored suit covered wide shoulders and an impressive chest. A gray-and-red silk necktie, perfectly knotted and aligned, fit snugly between starched collar points. Above, his face was freshly shaven, and that thick shock of expertly cut black hair was brushed away from his face, every strand in place. Still, despite the civilized trappings and controlled demeanor, there was something raw and untamed about Jake Taggart. Something wild.

Seen against the brilliant sunshine beyond the glass, the chiseled clarity of his profile made Susannah's breath catch and intensified the funny feeling in her stomach. He wasn't exactly handsome. His features were too strong for that. But he was utterly and compellingly masculine.

He was, Susannah realized, a perfect example of the alpha male—confident, in command, dominant, exuding an aura of awesome power and personal magnetism.

Yes, she thought shakily, now she understood why all the female employees, particularly the unmarried ones, found Jetco's C.E.O. endlessly fascinating. At lunch only the day before, the women had gone on and on about him.

"Wait until you see him, Susannah," one had said. "He's so rugged looking. I swear, I get goose bumps whenever he walks by my desk."

"Yep. Tall, dark and dangerous," another said with a sigh. "Works for me every time."

"Yeah, and his bod isn't bad, either."

"Oh, mercy. Can you imagine that man naked? Or what kind of lover he'd be?" The woman, a clerk in accounting, rolled her eyes and fluttered her hand against her chest. "Be still my heart."

"Well, personally, I think his most attractive feature is his eyes. They're so...so...hypnotic. I get all shivery inside whenever he looks at me," a young girl from the legal department added dreamily.

"Which, if you're lucky, may happen once a year," another woman drawled.

The rest of the lunch break the women had spent moaning over Jake's strict personal policy of nonfraternization. Though he apparently had an active social life, he made it a practice never to become involved, even casually, with any woman who worked for Jetco.

The tidbit of information had not affected Susannah one way or the other at the time, but now, looking at Jake Taggart's hard profile, she felt a profound relief. Accustoming herself to working for this overwhelming man was going to be difficult enough—provided, of course, that he let her keep the job—without the possible added complication of a personal relationship developing between them. The very thought sent a shudder through Susannah.

Jake ended his conversation and hung up the telephone. Refocusing his attention on Susannah, he picked up his line of questioning as though the interruption had not even occurred. "Now, then. You were about to tell me why you sought employment here."

"For...for the usual reason," Susannah stammered, looking confused.

"And that is?"

"Why...to earn a living."

Jake just looked at her. Yeah, right. He believed that. And pigs flew.

Who was she kidding? The Dushays didn't work for a living. With their money and power they didn't have to. And they looked down their patrician noses at the poor slobs who did. More than likely, she had gotten bored and decided it would be amusing to try her hand at a job for a while.

"I see. And who did you work for previously?"

She cleared her throat and shifted on the seat. "I was self-employed."

I'll just bet you were, Jake thought. With teas and charity fashion shows and cotillions at the country club, no doubt.

"Uh...Mrs. Pryor didn't seem to think my lack of experience would be a problem," Susannah added in a rush. "I learn fast and I'm a good worker. I promise you won't be sorry she hired me."

"Oh, I'm sure I won't be," he said with just a trace of irony. "I trust Alice's judgment completely."

Susannah breathed a sigh of relief. Jake gave her time to relax and settle back in her chair before he went on.

"Tell me, Miss Dushay. Where are you from?"

"Originally, from Zach's Corners. That's a small town in east Texas. About a hundred miles or so from here."

"Yes, I'm familiar with Zach's Corners." He paused a beat, holding her gaze. "Very familiar."

"Really? Then you've been there?"

"Oh, yeah. I've been there." Again he waited for her to make the connection, but there wasn't so much as a glimmer of recognition in her eyes.

Damn. He was beginning to think that she honestly didn't know who he was.

Jake sighed. He was disappointed, but he supposed he shouldn't be surprised. She couldn't be more than twenty-six, maybe twenty-seven. Which meant she'd been only somewhere around ten years old that summer. For that matter, he had only a vague recollection of her—dim memories of a big-eyed skinny kid he'd occasionally seen around town, usually in the company of her mother, Caroline Dushay, Nathan's young second wife.

Looking into Susannah's guileless face, Jake frowned. Either she hadn't known anything about the debacle, or she had forgotten it ... along with the Taggarts.

The very fact that she had accepted a job with his company tended to bear that out. If she'd known about what had happened and had half a brain, this would have been the last place she would have chosen to work.

Unless ... her father had put her up to it for some reason.

Even as the thought crossed his mind, Jake discounted it. He doubted that Nathan Dushay even remembered the Taggarts. They had been no more to him than a temporary nuisance, a bug to be squashed and scraped off the sole of his boot.

Jake let more than a minute lapse in taut silence, studying her. She really was an exquisite creature, he mused dispassionately. She had the bone structure and coloring of the Dushays, along with that finely textured skin that looked almost translucent. And that glorious blond hair streaked with silver. At present it was pulled away from her face with clips, but it was too thick and curly to tame completely. It rioted around the back of her head and shoulders in a silvery froth.

Medium brown arched brows and long lashes set off her green eyes. Her mouth was a bit too wide but it suited her. She had a softer, more vulnerable look than he associated with her family—probably a legacy from her mother—but there was no doubt that she was Nathan's daughter. He couldn't forget that.

Susannah shifted in her chair and cleared her throat. Jake was aware that he was making her nervous, and he drew a dark pleasure from the knowledge.

"I assume that Alice has explained your duties," he said suddenly, making her jump.

"I—I think so. I, uh...I'm to learn her job so that I can relieve her of some of her responsibilities."

"Alice has been with me since I formed the company," he continued. "She started out as my secretary, but now she's my administrative assistant. Her workload has grown steadily, but I couldn't persuade her to hire someone to help out. However, now that her husband has had a heart attack she no longer has a choice. Pete's fragile health forced him into retirement. Naturally, Alice wants to spend more time with him, and I think she should. However, to do that, she's going to have to cut back severely on her hours."

"Yes. I understand."

Jake deliberately let the silence stretch out again. Finally, he nodded. "Good. Now I'll let you get back to work." Standing, he again offered his hand across the top of the desk, and when she took it, he looked deep into her eyes. "Welcome aboard, Miss Dushay. I'm sure that our association will prove...interesting."

He felt the little shiver that ran through her and smiled. That's right, sweetheart, he thought with satisfaction. You're wise to be frightened of me.

Chapter Two

Darting an uneasy look at Jake, Susannah pulled her hand from his, murmured something about getting back to work and scurried for the outer office.

Jake watched her, his hard smile still in place. Her outstretched hand was only inches away from the knob when the door burst open and Grant Calloway strode in, clutching a fist full of papers.

"Jake, you got a minute to go over these—" Grant pulled up short, barely avoiding a collision with Susannah. "Oh. Sorry. I didn't know you were busy. I'll come back later," he said, backing away.

"Oh, no, please. Don't go on my account." Flashing a grateful smile, Susannah began to edge around him. "I was just leaving. Really."

"Grant, I don't believe you've met our newest employee," Jake said before Susannah could escape. "Susannah, this is Grant Calloway. He's the senior vice president and my second in command. He also happens to be my brother-in-law. Grant, meet Miss Dushay."

Turning to her with a charming smile, Grant took her hand. "It's a pleasure to mee—" He halted abruptly, his smile collapsing. He shot Jake a startled look. "Dushay? Did . . . did you say Dushay?"

"Yes. Susannah Dushay."

"I'm pleased to meet you, Mr. Calloway," Susannah murmured, but Grant didn't seem to hear her.

He stared from Jake to Susannah, then back to Jake. "You mean, the same Du—"

"Susannah is Alice's new assistant," Jake stated, fixing his brother-in-law with a hard look.

Grant hesitated. He clearly wanted to say more, but with admirable self-control he gathered his composure. "How do you do, Miss Dushay," he said smoothly, but this time his smile was stiff and he released her hand as quickly as courtesy allowed.

Puzzled, looking from one man to the other, Susannah mumbled something polite and excused herself.

The instant the door closed behind her, Grant shot across the room. "She *is* one of them, isn't she?" he demanded in an accusing tone. "One of the Zach's Corners Dushays."

Jake didn't turn a hair. "So it seems." He sat back down in the padded chair and withdrew some papers from his briefcase.

"What the hell is she doing here? Dammit, Jake! How could you hire that woman?"

"I didn't. Alice did."

"*Alice* hired her? Good Lord, man. Doesn't she know what happened?" Jake answered him with a steady look, and Grant rolled his eyes. "Ah, hell, don't tell me you haven't even *told* Alice?"

"Why should I have? I saw no reason for her to know."

"Jeez, you're the most secretive—" Grant cut off the angry retort and struggled for calm. "For one thing, she's been with you for nine years and she's a good friend. For another, if you had confided in her she would never have hired that woman.'' Grant paced away three steps, pivoted, and paced back, raking his fingers through his curly brown hair. ''Well, you'll just have to get rid of her,'' he said decisively.

''Don't worry, I will.''

Grant frowned at Jake's unconcerned tone. ''Why do I get the feeling that you're in no hurry?'' He leaned over the desk and braced both palms flat. His eyes narrowed on Jake's face. ''What are you up to?''

Jake leaned back in his chair and stared into the near distance, his expression thoughtful.

''Jake? Aw, hell. You're not thinking of taking advantage of this situation, are you? Tell me you're not.''

That drew a look and a lopsided grin. ''What's the matter, Grant? Don't you believe in fate? I do.''

''For Pete's sake, Jake, don't do anything you'll regret. Get rid of the woman now and forget the whole incident happened.''

''Forget?'' The word drew a snort of mirthless laughter. ''C'mon, Grant. We've been friends for...what? Sixteen years? By now you should know me better than that.'' His sardonic smile vanished and his eyes hardened. His voice dropped, the very softness of the low tones adding a chilling menace. ''When someone wrongs me or any member of my family, I don't forget. Not ever.''

For the space of three heartbeats, the two men's gazes locked—one searching, anxious, frustrated, the other hard with steely resolve.

Exhaling a sigh, Grant hung his head between his braced arms. ''I don't know why I bother. You always were a determined son of a—'' He bit off the epithet and raised worried eyes. ''I hope you know what you're doing.''

''Don't worry about it. I'll handle it. Now let's get down to business,'' he ordered, reaching for the lined yellow tablet. ''How did your meeting with Sanders and Nelson go?''

Grant sighed but began riffling through the papers he'd brought with him. When Jake used that tone, arguing was pointless.

They conferred for two hours, going over the newly acquired German contract to supply the Frankfurt company with Jetco's TZ computer chip and discussing progress on the new facility they were building in California.

When they finished, Jake informed Grant that he was sending him to Europe for a few months. "The Weissman deal was so profitable I'd like you to see what else you can drum up over there," he said casually. "Take Marianne with you. Make it a combination business trip and second honeymoon."

"What about Seth?" Grant asked dryly. "School won't be out for another couple of months, you know."

"He can stay with me. As soon as summer comes, I'll put him on a plane to join you."

Grant eyed him narrowly. "This has something to do with that Dushay woman, doesn't it? You want Marianne and me out of the way while you do whatever it is you're planning. Right?"

"It has to do with business," Jake replied evenly. "Now, why don't you call your wife and tell her to start packing?"

The expression on his brother-in-law's face shouted disapproval, but he kept his mouth shut and headed for the door.

"Oh, by the way... about Miss Dushay..."

Grant stopped with his hand on the doorknob and looked back at Jake. His hard expression held worry and wariness. "Yeah?"

"Don't say anything to Marianne or Seth about her. Miss Dushay isn't going to be here long. There's no reason they have to know."

Grant's expression grew harder. "I'm not going to tell them. But not because you ordered me not to. I love my wife and my son, and I don't want them upset."

Briefly, as Grant pulled the door shut behind him, Jake glimpsed Susannah in the outer office, standing bent over Alice's shoulder, her pale hair shimmering beneath the fluorescent lights.

When the door closed completely, Jake stared at it for several minutes. He still couldn't believe it. One of the Dushays, here. Working for him.

He rose and walked to the expanse of floor-to-ceiling glass that made up the two outer walls of his corner office and stared out. Forty floors below, sluggish traffic inched through downtown Houston and pedestrians bustled along the sidewalks. Skyscrapers formed canyon walls, casting the narrow streets in deep shadows.

Jake stood with his hands in his pockets, still as death, his chiseled features set. Only the glitter of his eyes betrayed the turbulence within. For the past two hours he had ruthlessly subdued his churning emotions and dealt with business, but now he gave them free rein.

Seventeen years. God, how often in all that time had he thought about something like this happening? Dreamed about it? Prayed for it?

Jake frowned. More in the beginning than lately, it was true, but he had never abandoned his goal. Always, the thought had hovered in the back of his mind.

For seventeen years he had lived for one thing: revenge.

Revenge for the pain, for the humiliation, for the demoralizing helplessness that had left the Taggarts stripped of even the smallest vestige of pride or dignity. Most of all, though, Jake wanted revenge for the heartbreak and shame his sister had suffered at the hands of the Dushays.

Marianne. Jake's nostrils flared and whitened, and his eyes narrowed. He didn't see the bustle of the city or the impressive skyline. His mind's eye focused on the past, and the events that had altered the lives of every member of his family.

His sister had been so innocent, so sweet...and so heartbreakingly young at the beginning of that long-ago summer. God, he didn't think he'd ever been that young. He'd sure as hell never been that trusting.

Whatever childish illusions he'd once possessed had been ripped away at an early age by harsh realities.

From the time she was born, though, he'd done his best to shield Marianne from that harshness. Someone had to; God knew his father hadn't bothered, or even been aware of the need.

To Jake, his mother and sister had seemed the only fine and decent things in an ugly world. Certainly, in those days, they'd been the only two people for whom he gave a damn. At an early age, Jake had willingly appointed himself Marianne's protector.

In school, he'd had no trouble shielding his little sister from the bullies and the cruelty of other children. A few fights, one or two bloody noses—after that it had taken only a hard look from him to make Marianne's classmates think twice about tormenting her. By the time he'd turned sixteen he had reached his full six-foot-one height, and no one, not even the adults, had dared to make snide remarks or look askance at Jake Taggart's sister. At least not within his hearing.

He hadn't kidded himself, though. Jake had always known what everyone thought of the Taggarts. One day he'd been in the grocery store picking up something for his mother when he'd overheard two women talking.

"Humph! Nothing but worthless trash, that's all they are and all they'll ever be. Will Taggart's drunker'n Cooter Brown most days. And that Jake! Why, those hard eyes of his make me shiver. If you ask me, with his attitude he's sure to end up in prison one day. You just mark my words."

The sentiment was one that had been shared by most of the townsfolk, but Jake had faced them all with an insolent air and a cold go-to-hell look that had made women and men alike give him a wide berth. He'd been the town "bad boy," the one all the mothers had warned their daughters about.

Beneath his mask of indifference Jake had seethed, but at least for him there had been ways to vent his rage. One had been The Blue Devil, the tavern where the sawmill hands gathered on Saturday nights after drawing their pay. Like most of the local youths, Jake had gone to work at the sawmill upon graduating from high school. Nearly all of what he'd earned had gone to his mother, but he'd usually been able to scrape together enough for a few beers. The Blue Devil drew a mean crowd, and a man looking to let off steam could always find a fight.

If that didn't do the trick, he found relief from the feelings that bedeviled him by spending a vigorous hour or so in the back of his rusty old pickup with a willing female—as often as not, one of Zach's Corners "respectable girls" out looking for excitement.

For Marianne there had been no such escape.

Jake's mouth hardened as memories of that long-ago summer flooded his mind. His sister had been barely sixteen, in the first lush bloom of young womanhood, innocent and shy and full of starry-eyed dreams of white knights and romance and a better life than the hard-scrabble existence that had always been their lot.

Perhaps if he had not protected her so much, if he had let her experience more of the cruelty of people, she would have been better off. As it happened, her trusting nature and innocent longing had made her ripe for the plucking...especially for someone like Philip.

Jake would never forget the shattered look on his sister's face when she had come to him and tearfully confessed that she was pregnant. Or the murderous rage he'd felt when she'd sobbed out that Philip Dushay was the father.

His jaw clenched and his hand tightened around the change in his pocket. The coins bit deep into his palm, but he didn't notice. Dammit, he'd warned her when Philip had first come sniffing around that he would break her heart. Jake hadn't minced words, either.

"I'm telling you, Marianne, he's a lying, cheating, scheming bastard, just like his old man! I've warned him not to come near you again."

"You had no right, Jake!" Marianne had wailed. "I'm old enough to decide for myself who I see."

"The hell you say. You stay away from that creep, you hear me. He's only after one thing, and if you think otherwise you're a fool. The Philip Dushays of this world sure as hell don't marry girls from The Swamp."

The Swamp. Jake's mouth twisted. God, he hadn't thought of that place in years. The appellation, given by the good folks of Zach's Corners to the area south of town, down in the river bottoms along Tobin Road, wasn't pretty but it was apt. In the summer months The Swamp was a sweltering steam bath, fit only for breeding snakes and mosquitoes and discontent. In the winter the fog rising from the river carried a humid chill that made a person ache to the marrow of his bones.

There, scattered among the loblolly pines and thickets, on small plots of marshy land, were the shanties and motley rusted-out trailer houses that were home to the town's poorer citizens.

Jake and Marianne had both been born in The Swamp, in the miserable four-room hovel their father had pieced together from scrap lumber, tin and tar paper. Their measly fifty acres of land, all that was left of Zachariah Taggart's original four-thousand-acre grant, had been in the family since 1822, when Jake's great-great-great grandfather had come to Texas with Stephen F. Austin and the original three hundred Anglo settlers.

Old Zach had prospered, and for over a century the Taggart name had stood for something in East Texas. Even the town, which had sprung up around the sight of his original plantation, had been named for him, but most folks had long since forgotten that.

Recent generations of Taggarts had not fared so well, and the family fortunes had steadily dwindled over the past sixty years. Coincidentally—or not so coincidentally, some thought—at the same time the Dushays' had begun to prosper.

Jake's father, Will Taggart, had worked as a handyman during his sober periods, which had occurred with less and less frequency as the years had gone by. It had been Leona, Jake and Marianne's mother—their gentle, patient, work-worn mother—who had supported the family by working as a cleaning woman for the Dushays and others like them.

Of course, no one in Zach's Corners had been quite equal to the Dushay family, Jake reminded himself with a cynical snort. From the beginning, when old Zachariah Taggart had built it, the mill had been the town's main industry and chief employer. It still was, only now it was owned by Nathan Dushay, along with the bank, the café, the hotel and two grocery stores. He and his family lived in an elegant house on a hill overlooking the town—far above riffraff such as the Taggarts.

Jake had been to the house many times to pick up his mother and save her the long walk home, but he had been inside only once—the night he had rammed his fist into Philip Dushay's handsome face.

Jake was fairly certain he'd broken Philip's nose, and even now, seventeen years later, the thought filled him with fierce satisfaction. He would have beaten the bastard to a bloody pulp if he'd had more time.

With his sister's heartbroken sobs still ringing in his ears, Jake had driven to the house on the hill in a blind rage. He had pounded on the front door with his fist, and when Caroline Dushay had opened it, he'd spotted Philip emerging from a room on the left of the foyer to see what had caused the commotion. Jake had brushed past the woman like a storm trooper and flattened Philip before he could react.

Unconsciously, Jake flexed his hand, experiencing again that painful but satisfying feel of flesh and cartilage smashing under his knuckles. The events of that evening were burned into his mind. Even after all this time, he could recall every detail.

Caroline had screamed as her stepson crashed to the marble floor of the entry hall with blood spurting from his nose.

With a snarl, Jake took a step forward and reached down to haul him to his feet, but as Philip tried to scramble away, whimpering, Nathan Dushay and Charles Goodwin, his lawyer and general flunky, rushed out of the study and grabbed Jake's arms.

"What the hell do you think you're doing?" Nathan demanded. "You can't just burst into my home and attack my son!" Twisting Jake's arm savagely behind his back, Nathan and Charles dragged him away from Philip. Jake bucked and kicked and tried to break free, but the two men held firm.

"Caroline, for God's sake, don't just stand there dithering. Call the sheriff!"

"Hold him, Dad. Don't let him get away. He's crazy," Philip whined. Climbing to his feet, he held a handkerchief to his nose and eyed Jake over the blood-splotched linen like a cornered fox.

"You slimy coward. I should have expected something like that from you," Jake raged. "Why don't you stand up and fight like a man?"

"Hey, you! Watch your mouth," Charles barked. "Nobody talks to a Dushay that way." By nature the attorney was a coward, but the favorable odds and a need to impress his boss had bolstered his nerve.

Jake stabbed him with a look. Old icy eyes glittered out of a nineteen-year-old face as unyielding as stone. Charles cleared his throat and looked away, his bluster withering.

"What's this all about?" Nathan demanded of his son. "What has he got against you?"

"I don't know. I swear it. He just burst in and hit me for no reason."

Jake lunged forward. "You lying bastard! You know why. You seduced my sister! I warned you to stay away from her but you sneaked around behind my back and fed her your sweet-talking lies. And when you got her pregnant you walked out on her!"

Nathan scowled. "Is that true, son?"

"Well…maybe." Philip shot Jake a resentful glare. Not quite meeting his father's eyes, he dabbed at his nose, his mouth sullen. "But she can't prove the kid's mine."

"Why you sorry—" Jake nearly succeeded in breaking free that time. It took the combined strength of both men to drag him back. "You know damned well you're the father!"

"Here now, you. Just calm down. Caro, forget that call to the sheriff," Nathan shouted to his wife. "We'll handle this little matter ourselves."

Caroline Dushay mumbled something into the receiver and replaced it. Wringing her hands, she stood to one side of the entryway and watched the four men.

Scowling, Nathan took a good look at Jake. "You're the Taggart boy aren't you?"

Jake turned his cold stare on the man. Nathan Dushay was thirty years older, twenty pounds heavier and three inches shorter than he was. A fleshy face and dark circles under his eyes testified to a lifetime of excess. "My name is Jake Taggart. And I'm not a boy."

"Dammit, Philip," Nathan growled, paying not the slightest notice to Jake's proud defiance. "What the hell were you thinking of, taking up with the Taggart girl? Haven't you got any sense?"

"What's the big deal? She's just Swamp trash. Anyway, I made sure we met secretly. You don't think I'd be seen in public with someone like that, do you?"

"You sorry sonofabitch!" Jake lunged again, his teeth bared in a feral snarl. Philip jumped back in panic.

"Hey, man, what do you want from me? I offered her money for an abortion but she turned it down. Anyway, look who's pointing a finger," he sneered. "The stud of Anderson County."

"Damn you! I may not be an angel but I've never seduced an innocent girl in my life."

"Innocent, ha! That's what you claim."

"And what you know, you bastar—"

"All right, Taggart, that's enough. Just cool off and get on back down the hill where you belong."

"But, Nathan, the girl..."

"Shut up, Caro," her husband growled. "Stay out of this."

His face a livid mask, Jake glared at the older man. "I'm not going anywhere until we settle this."

"It is settled. You heard Philip. He offered her money but she refused. What else can he do?"

"He can marry her," Jake snarled.

"Marry her? My son? Marry a little tramp from The Swamp?" Nathan laughed, a vile, insulting sound that nearly sent Jake over the edge. If he could have gotten his hands around the man's neck he would have killed him.

"Damn you. That spineless piece of dung isn't fit to kiss my sister's feet!"

Nathan glanced at his assistant and jerked his head toward the open front door. "Come on, Charles. I've heard enough. Let's show this trash out."

Cursing, Jake struggled and tried to dig in his heels, but he was no match for two men. The next thing he knew he went tumbling down the veranda steps. He ended up sprawled on his back in the circular front drive.

With Philip and Charles flanking him, Nathan stood on the top step with his feet braced wide, hands on his hips. His mouth curled contemptuously.

"Given the circumstances, Taggart, I'm willing to overlook your attack on my son. This once. But I'm warning you, if you ever lay a hand on him again, or if that slutty sister of yours tries to make a claim on Philip, you're going to be in big trouble. You hear me, boy?"

"It's not over," Jake snarled. Glaring back at Nathan's arrogant face, he got to his feet and wiped his hands on the seat of his pants. "You hear me, Dushay? This isn't the end of it."

It had been the end of it, though. Nathan had seen to that. Jake's jaws clenched as bitterness surged through him, as fresh and corrosive as it had been all those years before. He had been full of rage and righteous ire, but a penniless boy of nineteen had no chance against the richest, most influential man in three counties.

That had been the bitterest pill of all: the helplessness. There had been nothing he could do, no way to strike back—until now.

Slowly, Jake turned away from the window, and his pensive stare fixed on the closed door again.

It had to be Providence. Nathan's daughter had fallen into his hands like a ripe plum. He certainly wasn't going to ignore the Fates.

She didn't know it, but Susannah was going to be the instrument of his revenge against Nathan and Philip Dushay.

* * *

The heat hit Susannah like a suffocating wet blanket the instant she stepped from the city bus. As usual on the east side of town, a noxious odor hung in the air, courtesy of the paper mill and chemical and petroleum plants to the southeast. Air brakes hissed and the bus rumbled away into the night, adding the stench of diesel fumes to the polluted air.

Susannah darted a nervous glance around, then squared her shoulders and started walking. Holding tight to the shoulder strap on her purse, she hummed a brave tune under her breath and kept her eyes peeled.

She hated getting home after dark. The old section of town she lived in had only a few streetlights, and most of those had been broken long ago.

Susannah stumbled and cursed. Enormous trees lined the streets and formed canopies over them. They gave the seedy old neighborhood a semipicturesque look by day but at night cast shadows that made negotiating the cracked and buckled sidewalks treacherous. Half-expecting someone to jump out from behind a tree and grab her at any second, Susannah ignored the pitfalls and covered the three blocks from the bus stop to her home at a pace just under a run.

The front gate in the chain-link fence screeched when she pushed it open and stepped into the yard. Instantly, before she could relatch it, the porch light came on and the door on Marta's side of the duplex opened.

"Where in the world have you been? I've been worried sick about you, child. You've never gotten home this late before," her friend and landlady exclaimed, bustling down the walk in a flutter of gauzy drapery. Given her six-foot height and majestic build, Marta resembled a ship under full sail.

"I've only been working at Jetco a week, Marta," Susannah chided tiredly. "Anyway, I told you the job requires long hours. That's why it pays so well. But I am sorry if I worried you. I'll try to call the next time I have to work late." She trudged up the rickety steps to the small porch and let herself into her side of the duplex. Marta followed right on her heels.

Dumping her purse on the first available surface, Susannah stepped out of her shoes and collapsed into the room's only easy chair, propping her feet up on the cracked vinyl hassock. The chair was sprung and threadbare, but Susannah groaned with ecstasy as its familiar shape cushioned her exhausted body. With her head lolling against the high back, she contemplated her throbbing feet, flexing them experimentally. After years of working at home, usually in jeans and sneakers, wearing high heels everyday was sheer torture. She was beginning to think that was the toughest part of the job.

Then she remembered her boss and the way his gaze had followed her all day, and she quickly revised her opinion.

"Well? Did you meet him?"

Susannah looked up to find Marta standing over her, her arms crossed beneath her enormous bosom. "Meet who?"

"The Scorpio man, of course." At Susannah's blank look Marta gave a disgusted snort. "I told you this morning that according to your chart you would meet a tall dark Scorpio man today, one who would have a dramatic effect on your life. Don't tell me you forgot."

"No, of course not. It just slipped my mind for a moment."

Actually, she hadn't been listening. Susannah vaguely recalled Marta dogging her steps that morning as she'd rushed around getting ready for work, jabbering something about Venus and Pluto being trined or squared or some such gibberish. Knowing that Jake Taggart was due back from Europe, Susannah had been in a dither over meeting him and worried that she'd miss her bus and be late, and she had tuned Marta out.

Quite often Susannah merely pretended to listen to Marta's forecasts. Not that she was scornful of her friend's ability; she simply wasn't sure if she believed in astrology—or if she wanted to.

Studying the stars had been a lifelong hobby of Marta's, and now, after working as a grocery checker for forty years, she supplemented her pension by plotting astrological charts.

As a child, Susannah had been fascinated by the mystical process, but in growing up she had learned that life could, and often did, deal out some hard knocks. Marta's accuracy rate was astoundingly high, but Susannah wasn't sure that she wanted to know what the future had in store.

That, of course, did not stop Marta. She had plotted Susannah's chart—and Susannah's mother's, until her death the month before—daily for the past seventeen years, ever since they'd moved into the duplex.

"Well?" Marta demanded. "Tell me about him."

"There's nothing to tell." Susannah sniffed the air. "What's that delicious smell?"

"Goulash. When I realized you were going to be late, I brought some over and put it on your stove to keep warm. And don't change the subject. What do you mean, there's nothing to tell? There has to be. The stars are never wrong."

"Well, I'm sorry. The only man I met today was my boss." Susannah hauled herself out of the chair and padded into the tiny kitchen. Marta followed. "Oh, yeah, and his brother-in-law, Grant Calloway," she added, sniffing appreciatively at the aromatic steam that rose from the pot when she lifted the lid. "He's the vice president of Jetco."

"Brother-in-law? You mean he's married?"

"Uh-huh. To Mr. Taggart's sister." Susannah filled a plate with crackers and ladled goulash into a bowl. As she sat down at the table, Marta poured a glass of milk and put it at her place.

"You can count him out, then. Your Scorpio is definitely available."

Susannah's spoon halted midway to her mouth. "Oh, no. Are you saying this man and I are going to become *romantically* involved?"

"There's a strong possibility, yes."

"Well, I hope you're wrong. I don't have time for that sort of thing right now."

It wasn't an outright lie but neither was it the whole truth. The very idea of a romantic involvement made her uneasy, even though, deep inside, she yearned for someone to love, someone who would love her back.

"And when have you ever had time? Just tell me that." With a dramatic flutter of chiffon, Marta sat down opposite Susannah and placed her plump forearms on the table. "I've known you since you were ten years old, and in all that time you've had exactly five dates. And four of those were while you were still in high school, before your mother took sick. I practically had to get out a whip and a chair to make you go out with that young teacher you met at business school."

"Mother was ill. I couldn't—"

"I know, I know." Marta silenced her with an upraised hand. "You had to take care of her. We'll overlook, for the moment, the fact that I was available to stay with Caroline anytime you needed me."

"Oh, Marta, I never meant to slight you," Susannah said quickly, experiencing a wave of guilt. "You've been like family to Mother and me ever since we moved in, and I appreciate all you've done for us. Truly. But I just—"

"Yes, I know. You felt it was your place to look after your mother." Marta sighed and shook her head, making wispy strands of dyed red hair float about her round face and her four-inch-long dangling earrings sway and clank. "You're a good person, Susannah—an unselfish, giving person. Maybe too giving."

"Marta!"

"Now, now. Don't go getting all upset," the older woman soothed. She patted Susannah's hand and met her wounded look lovingly. "All I'm saying, child, is you have a tendency to always put everyone else's needs before your own, no matter what. You're twenty-seven years old. For the past ten years, ever since Caroline's illness was diagnosed, I've watched you make one sacrifice after another.

"First you dropped out of college and went to business school instead so you could start supporting the two of you. Then, instead of getting a job where you'd at least be with other people and have some kind of life, what did you do? You started a secretarial service so you could work at home and nurse your mother at the same time. Why, for the past six years you've practically been a prisoner in this house, never getting out or making friends, never having any fun." Marta paused dramatically and lowered one eyelid, her voice dropping to a naughty whisper. "Never being seduced by a man."

At once, her teasing demeanor vanished and she fixed Susannah with a stern look. "It's neither right nor healthy for a lovely young woman like you to live like a recluse."

"What else could I do? She was my mother."

Marta sighed again. "Knowing you, nothing. You were a good daughter to Caroline. No one can fault you for that. But, child, your mother's gone now. Except for going to that office every day, you're still stuck in a rut. It's time— past time if you ask me—for you to get out and have a life of your own."

Unable to meet her friend's level gaze, Susannah stared at the bowl of goulash she was needlessly stirring. She knew Marta was right; she wanted a life of her own and someone she could give her heart to—she really did. The trouble was, Susannah was honest with herself, brutally so, and she knew she was vulnerable.

Not for a moment did she resent the time she had spent caring for her mother, but those ten barren years had left her lonely and starved for love. She was terrified of that hunger, afraid of where it might lead. She could not afford to make a mistake when giving her heart. Her character, her disposition, her personality, almost everything about her, Susannah had inherited from her mother, and she feared that, like Caroline, she was one of those women who fell in love only once. She did not want to end up like her mother, alone and brokenhearted because she had fallen in love with the wrong man.

"Mother is gone, it's true, but you're forgetting there's still that mountain of medical bills that has to be paid."

"So? Falling in love won't stop you from doing that." Not giving her a chance to reply, Marta sat forward eagerly. "Now then, tell me about this boss of yours."

Susannah choked on a mouthful of goulash. She coughed and sputtered and dabbed at her streaming eyes for a full minute. When she finally recovered, she shook her head emphatically. "Oh, no. I know what you're thinking and you couldn't be more wrong. There could never be anything like that between Jake Taggart and me. It's impossible."

Though fascinating in a dangerous sort of way, Jake Taggart was too intense, too dominant and powerful for her. Even if she could attract him, which seemed so unlikely it was laughable, she would never be able to hold her own with a man like Jake. No, what she needed was someone gentle and caring who would cherish her.

"When is his birthday?"

"Marta, I'm telling you the Scorpio man—if there is one—definitely isn't Jake."

"You're sure about that, are you? Scorpio men are easy to spot, you know. Why don't you tell me about him?"

"No. Believe me, it would be a waste of time."

Marta cocked her head to one side and eyed Susannah shrewdly. "Okay. Then I'll describe the typical Scorpio male and you can tell me if it fits.

"Let's see now. He's confident and determined. He's a man who knows exactly who and what he is, and he's very aware of his own strengths and weaknesses. When he sets his sights on something, he will move heaven and earth to reach his goal, and he'll usually succeed.

"He's secretive to a fault, but bluntly honest. If you ask his opinion he'll give it, so if you can't take the unvarnished truth, don't ask. On the other hand, if he gives a compliment, you can be sure he means every word.

"He's reserved—usually doesn't say much. He's quite formidable, actually. He makes a bad enemy, but an intensely loyal friend. He never forgets a slight *or* a favor. And when wronged, he always gets even. In spades.

"The Scorpio male is always in control, never shows his feelings or appears nervous. Even so, there's an awesome inner strength and energy about him that's almost palpable.

"As far as physical traits go, he would have an arresting appearance, with clearly drawn facial features and a powerful physique. And probably heavy eyebrows and plenty of hair on his arms and legs. But the most distinctive feature of all about a Scorpio is his eyes. They're hypnotic. So intense they seem to stab right through you."

Susannah's spoon clattered against the bowl.

A smug smile played around Marta's mouth. "Why, Susannah honey, whatever's the matter? You're downright pale."

Chapter Three

The next morning Susannah sailed into the Jetco Building with her shoulders squared and her chin high, her spiked heels tapping briskly against the marble floor of the lobby. She looked efficient and confident in her new teal suit, which was why she had worn it. Not that she *needed* a confidence booster. She wasn't worried.

Admittedly, the night before, when Marta had described a Scorpio male, Susannah had experienced something close to panic, but the sensation had lasted only a moment, just long enough for her practical nature to reassert itself.

So what if the list of traits and physical features fit Jake to a T? It was coincidence. Pure coincidence. That was all. There were probably thousands of men in Houston who fit the same profile. Surely not all of them were Scorpios.

When the elevator doors opened, Susannah squeezed inside with the rest of the waiting crowd and fixed her eyes on the floor indicator. All right. Okay. So she had experienced some sort of strange sensation—a constriction in her chest—whenever he'd come near, or whenever she'd caught him staring at her. That didn't mean anything, except that he made her nervous.

Susannah did not completely dismiss Marta's prediction—her friend had been on target too many times for that—but she flatly refused to consider, even for a moment, that her own personal Scorpio could be Jake Taggart. She was a novice where men were concerned, a mere babe in the woods. Jake was too intense, too dominant, too…too rawly male for her to handle. The very idea made Susannah shiver. Whether the reaction sprang from fear or excitement she didn't know, but she wasn't going to find out. Jake Taggart was out of her league, and she wasn't a fool to go asking for trouble.

Despite her firm resolve, Susannah experienced a fresh surge of uneasiness moments later when she entered the office and came face-to-face with the object of her thoughts.

Jake stood before Alice's desk, riffling through a stack of mail. When she jerked to a halt just inside the door, he looked up, straight into her eyes. Susannah's heart lurched.

Beneath lazy lids, his gray eyes burned with a quiet intensity. He looked sensational in an impeccable charcoal gray suit, starched shirt and silk tie, but the civilized attire in no way muted his ruggedness. The aura of dangerous male that he exuded hit her like a physical blow.

Slowly, he subjected her to one of his thorough scrutinies, setting off a chain reaction of quivering nerves and pounding pulses within Susannah. His gaze swept over her from the top of her head to her suede pumps. Susannah held her breath, and her heart tapped against her ribs.

When done, Jake nodded, bid her a brusque, "Good morning," and disappeared into his office. Susannah was left staring after him, dazed and off balance, her poor heart still thumping.

At noon, a stunning redhead arrived at the office. To Susannah's chagrin, Jake and the woman left arm in arm for lunch, their heads close together in intimate conversation. Slack-jawed, she stared after them for a full five seconds before dissolving into a fit of giggles. So much for her ridiculous fears.

Two days later Jake's luncheon companion was a blonde.

The following week, Susannah, Alice and Jake were working late one night when a luscious brunette, draped in diamonds and a designer evening gown, sauntered into the office and reminded him that they had only twenty minutes to make the curtain at Jones Hall.

Within ten, Jake had changed into a tuxedo he kept in his office closet and they were on their way.

Feeling utterly foolish but vastly relieved, Susannah dismissed Marta's prediction completely.

Peace of mind on that score, however, did not alter her reaction to Jake. He continued to make her nervous and on edge. Her skin prickled and breathing became difficult whenever he came near her. To be perfectly fair, he was always polite, never raising his voice or making unreasonable demands. Lately he had even made a few friendly overtures. But with just a look from those piercing eyes he could send her composure flying...and it seemed to Susannah that every time she looked up, Jake was watching her.

He was open about it. Instead of looking away and pretending interest elsewhere, as most people would, or showing embarrassment over having been caught staring, he boldly held her gaze until she was the one who became flustered and broke eye contact.

On a personal level, Susannah didn't now what to make of the intense, enigmatic man, but when it came to business she quickly realized that Jake Taggart was a dynamo. The first day, she had assumed that his prolonged absence from the office and the need to catch up had been responsible for their workload, but as time went on, it became apparent that the demanding pace Jake set was normal.

Dorothy Haskins, Jake's secretary, handled the routine correspondence and clerical work, but anything of a confidential or sensitive nature was Alice's responsibility, one which she promptly turned over to Susannah.

Under Alice's tutelage Susannah was slowly learning the computer business and how Jetco operated. However, after two weeks she was no more comfortable around Jake than she had been the day they met.

Though the coldness she had detected during their initial meeting was no longer in evidence, she was determined not to give him any cause to dismiss her. Susannah worked like a demon, staying late most nights, working through her lunch hour, doing whatever was needed without comment or complaint.

By the end of the second week she was so tired, when quitting time came and she heard sounds of the other employees departing, she was more than ready to join them.

Susannah quickly put away the files she'd been working on and took her purse from the desk drawer. Halfway across the office she hesitated and glanced back at Jake's closed door. She wasn't keen on disturbing him, but Alice had left early that afternoon to take her husband to the doctor for a checkup and Susannah didn't feel right about walking out without a word and leaving the office empty. Reluctantly, she retraced her steps and tapped on Jake's door.

Five minutes later she was back at the computer typing a letter that he wanted to go out that night.

It was dark by the time Susannah finished, and as she left the building, her bus was pulling away from the curb.

"Hey, wait! Wait!" she yelled, chasing after it, but all she got for her trouble was a face full of diesel fumes and her legs and skirt splattered with muddy water.

In typical Texas fashion, the weather had done an aboutface. The day had started out hot and muggy, and Susannah had dressed accordingly, but since she had gone out at noon, a late spring norther had roared in, bringing gusty winds and rain and dropping the temperature by at least fifty degrees.

With her lightweight challis skirt whipping about her legs, Susannah huddled under the inadequate protection of the bus shelter, shivering and rubbing her arms through the thin sleeves of her rain-splattered blouse.

Stamping her feet, she shifted from one to the other and peered through the rain and glare of headlights for another bus, though she knew the next one wasn't due for twenty minutes.

Motor traffic zipped by, tires swishing, white and red lights reflecting on the wet paving. A taxi pulled up in front of the next building, and a man with an umbrella dashed out and scrambled inside. A passing vagrant paused to take a long pull from a wine bottle, then staggered on, oblivious to the frigid wind and rain. Otherwise, the sidewalks were deserted.

Susannah glanced around and hugged herself tighter. She was cold, she was tired, she was hungry...and she was growing more uneasy by the moment. A woman alone in downtown Houston after dark was an easy target.

Over the patter of rain she heard an engine whine as a car spiraled down the ramp of the Jetco parking garage. The exit ramp fed onto the side street, and a moment later, a low-slung sports car shot around the corner and zoomed past. A few yards away the driver slammed on the brakes and put the car in reverse.

Susannah's heart began to pound and her chest squeezed.

When the car backed up even with her, the shadowy figure inside leaned across the seat and flung the passenger door open. Susannah backed up a step. Frantically, she looked around for an avenue of escape.

"Susannah? What are you doing out here?"

Shock brought her to a standstill, her eyes widening. "Mr. Taggart?" Bending, Susannah peered into the car. "Is that you?"

"What are you doing standing around on the street corner in the rain after dark?" he demanded, ignoring her question.

"Why... I—I'm waiting for my bus."

He shot her a sharp look, frowning. Then he gestured for her to get into the car. "Come on, I'll take you home."

"Oh, I couldn't let you do that!" Whatever scant relief she had experienced when she realized he wasn't a pervert intent on molesting her, vanished in a blink. The thought of being confined in that tiny car with her boss brought Susannah close to panic. "I... I'm sure I don't live anywhere near you, and I wouldn't want to take you out of your way."

"It's no problem."

"But... I—I'm all wet and muddy. I'll ruin your upholstery."

He stabbed her with one of his patented looks. "Get in the car, Susannah. I'm taking you home."

Left with no choice, Susannah swallowed hard and stepped from the dubious protection of the bus shelter into the sleek sports car.

The inside of the car smelled of leather, citrusy aftershave and a subtle male scent that made her nose twitch. Mingling with the pleasant odors were the smell of rain and cold that clung to her skin and clothing.

She huddled in the bucket seat with her arms crossed over her midriff, her hands rubbing her upper arms and elbows. The damp blouse stuck to her skin in large splotches. Susannah shivered in the stream of warm air from the car's heater. Her eyes remained fixed on the dash and away from the driver. She was so tense it was a moment before she noticed that the car had not budged. Warily, she slanted a

glance Jake's way, and jumped when she found him staring at her.

He cocked one eyebrow, his mouth curving with a hint
of amusement. "Would you like to tell me where you live?"
he asked with lazy sarcasm, and Susannah felt heat climb
her neck.

She managed to stammer out directions, then fell silent
and stared straight ahead as the engine purred and the sleek
vehicle eased out into traffic.

Susannah felt utterly foolish. He knew he rattled her. He
probably knew why, as well. She gritted her teeth to stifle a
groan. Lord, she was pathetic, a classic case of a love-
starved virgin all atremble in the presence of raw mascu-
linity.

"Are you having car trouble?"

Susannah reacted to the deep rumble of Jake's voice as
though it were a clap of thunder, starting so hard she almost cleared the seat. "Par-pardon me?"

"I assume you were taking the bus because your car is
out of commission."

"Oh. No, I don't have a car."

He shot her an incredulous look. "You don't own a car?
How the hell do you get around?"

For once Jake's cool demeanor had been knocked for a
loop, which, strangely, restored Susannah's composure
somewhat. "I take the bus. Or once in a while, if I have a
real emergency, I borrow my landlady's car. But it's an old
'59 De Soto and not very reliable, so I don't like to drive it
too far."

Houston was notorious for its lack of decent public
transportation, but Susannah didn't think her disclosure
warranted the reaction she was getting from Jake. He
looked at her as though she were some alien being he'd
never encountered before.

"How long have you been without a car?" he asked, shooting her another frowning glance as he turned a corner.

"All my life. Well...since my mother and I moved here, anyway. That was seventeen years ago."

That drew another sharp look. Susannah's uneasy feeling returned. She shifted in her seat and transferred her gaze to the passing traffic.

Jake drove on in brooding silence, a frown knitting his brow. "So...you and your mother moved here seventeen years ago," he said casually after a few moments. "What happened to your father? Is he deceased?"

"No. My parents divorced when I was ten. That's when Mother and I came here to live, mainly because job opportunities were better." And because her father had made it impossible for her mother to remain in Zach's Corners, Susannah added silently.

"I see," Jake murmured, but his tone and puzzled frown indicated just the opposite. "Do you see your father often?"

Susannah's hesitation lasted only a second. "No. Not very often. We've...sort of grown apart."

Actually, they had never been close, but since the divorce the chasm between them had widened. Susannah suspected that her father would never forgive her for choosing her mother over him.

Silence once more descended. Several moments passed before the unfamiliar surroundings registered on Susannah. She sat up straighter and looked around.

"Where are we? This isn't the way to my house."

"I know. First we're going to have dinner."

"Oh, no. Please. That's not necessary. Really."

"Sure it is. After the way I've been working you it's the least I can do," he said affably, and to her astonishment, he slanted her a smile that made her toes curl. "Besides, I'm starving, so I know you must be, too."

"Oh, but—"

"Relax, Susannah." He said her name in a low growl that sent her racing heart into overdrive. "I know this quiet little restaurant that serves great food. You'll love it."

"But . . . I can't go into a restaurant like this." She gestured toward her splattered skirt and stockings, her voice edging upward with real panic. "I'm covered with mud."

"Hmm." He gave her a quick once-over. "All right, then. No restaurant." Susannah sagged with relief, but even as she exhaled a long sigh he whipped the car into the drive-through lane of a fast-food place. "If it'll make you feel better we'll get take-out."

Renewed panic slammed through Susannah, but before she could object, Jake pulled up to the speaker and ordered a bucket of fried chicken and all the trimmings.

Within minutes they were zipping along Interstate 10 toward her east Houston neighborhood.

Except for the jittery sensation in her stomach, a numbing feeling of unreality enveloped Susannah. She heard the pelting on the roof of the car and the rhythmic thump of the wipers sweeping the rain from the windshield, she heard herself answer Jake's questions, she saw the familiar landmarks along the way, she smelled the savory aroma wafting from the sacks stowed behind the seat, but none of it really registered. Her mind simply could not accept what her senses were telling her: she was in a car that cost more than she made in two years, being driven by her boss—a man who scared the daylights out of her—to her home, where he apparently intended for them to share a bucket of take-out chicken at her rickety kitchen table. It was all simply too bizarre to take in.

Unbelievably, Jake seemed to see nothing out of the ordinary about the situation. If anything, he appeared more relaxed and comfortable than she had ever seen him.

Before getting behind the wheel he had removed his suit coat, and as he drove he loosened the knot in his tie and slipped it off. Then he unfastened the top three buttons on his shirt, removed his cuff links and rolled up his sleeves. Gripping the steering wheel loosely, he settled back in the leather seat in a lazy sprawl that was somehow thoroughly and enticingly masculine.

The subtle ripple of muscle and tendon just beneath the skin drew Susannah's gaze to his forearms, with their liberal dusting of silky black hair. Helplessly, she stared at his broad wrists, those capable, beautifully shaped hands, the long blunt fingers flexing around the leather-covered steering wheel. A car horn honked, and Susannah jerked her gaze away.

Jake kept the conversation going by asking polite questions about her family and prodding her now and then for directions. Susannah answered automatically, barely aware of doing so. If he noticed the vagueness and brevity of her replies or her distracted air he didn't let on.

The closer they got to her house, the more tense she became. When she saw the bus pulling away from her stop she panicked. "I—I'm not really very hungry. Why don't you just let me out here and I'll walk the rest of the way," she said in a rush.

"Don't be silly. It's a monsoon out there. Besides, I wouldn't think of letting you walk home alone on these dark streets."

"But I do it every night."

He slanted her a look that took her breath away. "Tonight you're with me. And I'm taking you home. Now which way?" His voice was soft but unyielding, like velvet-covered steel. In the light from the dash his gray eyes flashed with a strange proprietary gleam and arrogant male dominance.

Sighing, Susannah subsided against the seat and gave him directions. Somehow she had aroused his protective instincts. Even with her limited experience she knew that further argument was pointless against a forceful man like Jake.

When he brought the car to a halt at the curb, he sat motionless, staring thoughtfully at the duplex. On Marta's side the curtain over the front window twitched.

"It's really not safe to park an expensive car like this one on the street in this neighborhood."

Jake turned to her, his eyes glittering beneath half-closed lids, and smiled wryly. "Trying to get rid of me, Susannah?"

"No! No, of course not," she lied too quickly, and his smile deepened into a chuckle.

"Well, don't worry about it. I doubt that car thieves or chop-shop boys are working on a night like this."

Jake came around to her side with an umbrella, but it offered scant protection from the blowing rain. By the time they dashed to the porch they were half-soaked and shivering.

From the corner of her eye, Susannah saw Marta's door ease open a tiny crack. She hurriedly unlocked her side of the duplex and ushered Jake inside.

A blast of warmth hit them when they stepped into the dark living room. Marta, bless her, had come over and fired up the furnace. She might be a busybody, Susannah thought affectionately, groping for the light switch, but she was still a dear.

When Susannah turned from switching on the lights, Jake was standing in the middle of the floor, looking around. As usual, his expression revealed nothing, but there was a puzzled look in his eyes.

Shifting from one foot to the other, Susannah folded her arms, unfolded them, then folded them again. Suddenly she saw her modest home through Jake's eyes—the shabbiness, the cramped rooms, the worn furnishings. Over the years she'd grown so accustomed to the place that she'd never really looked at it. She gnawed at her lower lip and watched him.

"How long did you say you've lived here?"

"Seventeen years. Ever since we moved here from east Texas."

He stopped in the archway that led into the dining room. The tiny room was crammed with file cabinets, a worktable and typewriter and the obsolete computer and printer she'd bought secondhand.

Jake glanced at her, and glanced back at the equipment. "You really were self-employed, weren't you?"

"Why, yes. I operated a secretarial service from here for the past seven years. Mostly I typed students' papers, reports and letters for small businesses—that sort of thing. I didn't make much money, but at least it allowed me to stay home."

She picked up the sacks of food he had placed on the coffee table and cut through the cluttered office, heading for the kitchen. The sooner she fed him, the sooner he would leave. Jake followed, and as she pulled place mats and napkins from the cabinet and set out the food, he leaned his hips against the counter and folded his arms, watching her.

"Why was staying home so important? I would have thought that you would've wanted to get out in the world, meet people. Men, in particular. A woman as beautiful as you shouldn't be cooped up at home all the time."

Susannah nearly dropped the soft drinks she was lifting from one of the sacks. Her startled gaze flew to his face, and her heart began to pound at what she saw. She could hardly believe he'd called her beautiful. Especially not in that caressing tone. Yet his bold stare told her otherwise. Something glittered in the gray depths of those mesmerizing eyes—something hot and sensuous, something dangerous. His expression was one of frank male interest.

"You are very beautiful, you know. I'm surprised some man hasn't already carried you off."

The last was said in a low, husky pitch that stroked her nerve endings like warm velvet.

Flustered, Susannah ducked her head and went back to setting out their meal. Scalding heat rose up her neck and flooded her cheeks, and her hands shook. She had no doubt that Jake had spotted the telltale reactions, but all she could do was tough it out and pretend to be unaffected.

"I didn't have time for men." She addressed the remark to her hands, which were fumbling to pry the lid off a carton of gravy. "About ten years ago my mother was diagnosed as having a degenerative muscular disease. It progressed rapidly, and within three years she needed constant care. Working at home allowed me to look after her and support us, as well. Of course, I didn't make much money, and the bills piled up, but we managed."

"I see." Jake's voice was still soft, but this time the husky tones were laced with compassion. "I'm sorry, Susannah. I didn't know about your mother."

Susannah glanced at him and found he was studying her intently, his expression thoughtful. His compassion was almost as unsettling as the dark emotion she'd seen in his face only moments before. She fiddled needlessly with the containers of food. "That's all right. You couldn't have known."

Trying for a bright smile, she gestured for him to take a seat.

The scarred and wobbly table and three bentwood chairs had been a junk-store find for which Susannah had paid twenty dollars. She had sanded and painted them a cheery yellow, but their poor quality and battered condition were still obvious. Before tonight it had never bothered her, but now she was acutely conscious of her home's every shortcoming.

The chair squeaked under Jake's weight when he took his place at the table. She prayed it would support him through the meal. He didn't appear uncomfortable, but she wondered what he thought.

"I take it your mother died recently," Jake prodded when they had served themselves.

"Yes. About six weeks ago." Susannah tried to sound unaffected, but her voice quivered. Even though she had known her mother's passing was inevitable, even though she was grateful that at least now her suffering was over, Susannah still felt the sharp pain of loss. Just thinking of her gentle mother brought a sheen of tears to Susannah's eyes and caused her throat to ache.

From the look in his eyes, Susannah knew that Jake was aware of her distress but, displaying a sensitivity she found surprising, he made no comment. Instead, he murmured a polite, "That's too bad. I'm sorry," and picked up his fork.

He dug into his food with gusto, giving Susannah a few minutes to pull herself together before picking up the conversation again.

"So... I take it you haven't had time for much of a social life for the past ten years," he said, plucking another piece of chicken from the bucket.

"Not much, no."

None was closer to the truth, but she wasn't about to admit that to him. Somehow, she didn't think a man who dated a bevy of beautiful women in the space of one week would understand.

Besides, she didn't want to discuss her personal life with Jake. It made her uncomfortable. *He* made her uncomfortable. Something about Jake frightened and fascinated her all at the same time. She didn't understand it, but strange warning bells went off whenever he came near her, and she got all jittery inside. She just wanted him to eat his dinner and leave, before she said or did something that would make her look like a fool.

The whole situation was unreal. He was her boss, for heaven's sake. Plus he was a wealthy, important man who owned his own company. She couldn't believe that he was actually sitting at her kitchen table eating take-out chicken. Why, his suit alone cost more than the entire contents of her duplex.

"And now?" Jake wiped his greasy fingers on a napkin and waited for her answer, his eyes once again intent on her.

"Now?" Susannah blinked. Somehow she had lost track of the conversation. Something about him—perhaps his alert stare or the sudden air of expectancy about him—set the warning bells to clanging louder than ever. He looked like a hungry mountain lion about to pounce on an unsuspecting doe.

"Do you have time in your life for men now? Or rather, I should say, a man."

The strange tightness gripped her chest like a vice. "I...I really haven't thought about it."

"Then think about it now."

"Well, I..." Susannah put down her chicken and dabbed at her lips with her napkin. "I suppose . . . that is, if I have time . . . but as you know, my hours are so unpredictable. . . . Not that I'm complaining, mind you. It's just that—"

"Susannah." Jake said her name in a soft rasp that made her scalp tingle. "I don't want to talk about work." His hypnotic gaze held her captive, his eyes searing into her soul. He reached across the table and placed his hand on her arm, and his touch seemed to brand her skin. "I want to talk about you." He waited a beat, then added softly, "And me."

Susannah went utterly still. She stared into his determined face, her heart booming like a kettledrum. "I . . . I don't understand."

"Don't you?"

Susannah shook her head slowly. For several agonizing moments he made no reply. He merely looked at her.

Then he rose and came around to her side of the table. Watching him, Susannah's eyes grew round with alarm. Yet when he bent and grasped her elbows she was powerless to stop him. As docile as a rag doll, she allowed him to lift her to her feet, her gaze all the while held captive by the determined glitter in his smoky eyes.

His arms enfolded her, and he pulled her close. His gaze slid down to her slightly parted lips, and his eyes darkened beneath half-lowered lids. "Then I'll explain it this way," he murmured in that warm velvet voice.

Susannah's eyes widened but all she had time to do was gasp before his hard mouth settled over hers.

Chapter Four

Shock held Susannah absolutely motionless. Her heart banged and her senses reeled. A hot flush washed over her from the soles of her feet to the roots of her hair.

The audacious kiss took her breath away. It was possessive, dominant and sure, and unbreakable. Jake held her tight, one big hand splayed between her shoulder blades, pressing her to him, the other arm wrapped around her waist.

New sensations overwhelmed Susannah. It was as though her senses had been dormant for years and had suddenly sprung to life. She could feel his heat, his hardness, all along the front of her body. Her breasts were flattened against his chest, and she felt the heavy beat of his heart in slow counterpoint to the mad pounding of her own. His scent was all around her, his taste on her tongue.

All during her teens and the long, barren years she had cared for her mother, Susannah had dreamed romantic dreams, dreams of being held in a man's arms, of being kissed and caressed, of the sweet pleasure she would feel.

But her dreams couldn't compare to the reality of Jake's kiss. There was nothing sweet or soft about the pleasure he was giving her. This was lush and raw and ardent.

It was all so new, so impossibly thrilling, Susannah could barely take it in. She felt on fire, and more alive than she had ever been in her life.

Confusion, excitement and fear coursed through Susannah in equal measure. The extremes of emotion wrung a small whimper from her, and Jake answered it with a low growl, a purely masculine sound that sent a shiver rippling over her skin.

At last Jake ended the kiss, but he did not loosen his hold on Susannah, which was just as well. She wasn't at all sure that her legs were capable of supporting her weight.

He raised his head slowly. His expression was strange, almost angry. His searching gaze probed her pale features one by one, her parted lips, still wet and slightly swollen from his kiss, her glazed eyes, the erratic pulse that fluttered just beneath her ear.

Susannah stared back, speechless. Her breath shuddered in and out, and she ran the tip of her tongue over her lips.

Homing in on the nervous action, Jake's eyes narrowed and darkened. With another growl, he lowered his head again.

This time his kiss held raw passion and hunger. His tongue plunged into her mouth and began a sensuous ravagement that sent fire streaking through Susannah and turned her body to mush. In and out, in and out—he enticed and inflamed with each slow stroke. Need built within Susannah, a wild hunger that terrified her and made her ache.

His hand slid from her waist to the base of her spine, and he rocked her hips against his, the undulating rhythm matching the slow, maddening strokes of his tongue.

His other hand plunged into the thick mane of curls and clasped the back of her head.

The devouring kiss excited Susannah almost beyond reason, but it frightened her, too. She could not handle the feelings he aroused in her; they were too strong, too intense. Nor did she trust Jake's passion. It was real—the evidence of that was unmistakable—but mixed with it, just below the surface, Susannah sensed a darker emotion.

A shudder rippled through her, a helpless response she was powerless to contain. It sprang in part from the ravaging need that threatened to render her senseless and in part from the leashed anger in Jake.

He felt the reaction and lifted his head. His gaze probed deep. Finally he loosed his hold and cupped her jaw. His eyes narrowed, and he swept his thumb across her lower lip, still wet from his kiss. "Think about it," he whispered.

With that, he released her and walked out.

Susannah swayed and had to grab the table to keep from falling. Shaken and speechless, she watched through the doorway as he strode through her cluttered office/dining room and disappeared into the living room and beyond. An instant later, over the heavy thudding of her heart and the strange roaring in her ears, she heard the front door close.

Lifting her hand, she put four shaking fingers over her mouth. "Oh, dear Lord."

She was still standing there, trembling, a moment later when the back door opened and Marta rushed inside.

"Let me guess," she began excitedly. "That hunk in the Porsche was your boss. Right?"

Susannah nodded, her dazed stare still fixed on the empty doorway.

"I knew it! I— Say, are you all right?" Marta frowned. "Wait a minute. Did that guy try something with you? Oh, God! He didn't hurt you, did he?"

"What? Oh." With an effort, Susannah dragged herself back to the present. "No. No, of course not. We worked late, and Mr. Taggart was kind enough to drive me home. That's all.''

"Uh-huh.'' Marta cast a droll look at the empty containers on the table, and Susannah shifted uneasily.

"We . . . we worked through dinner, so naturally . . .''

"Oh, naturally,'' Marta agreed. Her attention switched to Susannah, and she pursed her lips. "That Porsche must be one rough-riding car, though.'' She leaned in close and peered at Susannah's mouth. "What happened? Did you get thrown against the dash when he hit a pothole?''

"No. Why would you think that?''

Marta grinned. "Because your hair is mussed and your lips are swollen. Either you received a hard smack or, sweetie, you've just been kissed senseless.''

A scalding red blush crept up Susannah's neck. "It . . . it was just an impulse. It didn't mean anything.''

Marta threw back her head and laughed delightedly. "Oh, honey, don't you believe it. If your Mr. Taggart is a Scorpio—and I'd bet my pension that he is—that kiss meant something all right. Trust me . . . a Scorpio never acts on impulse.''

Seth had already gone to bed when Jake entered his penthouse apartment. Tossing his suit coat on the living room sofa as he passed it, he strode straight to the bar in the corner. He cast a sour look at the decanters of Scotch, bourbon and gin sitting on the bar and reached into the refrigerator beneath the counter for a bottle of mineral water.

Jake kept the hard stuff for the occasional guest, but he personally never touched it. Years before, when he had left home, he'd sworn off drinking. Jake had seen firsthand what alcohol could do to a man, and he'd wanted no part of it. He'd had things to accomplish, goals to reach, and he wasn't going to let anything—not anything—interfere.

Since the day he'd left home, he hadn't had so much as a beer.

It had been a wise decision, one he'd never regretted. Still, he had to admit . . . the way he felt at the moment, he could do with a good slug or two of something with a little punch to it.

Jake twisted the cap off and took a healthy swig of the bubbly water straight from the bottle. He grimaced at the taste and released a raspy breath.

Carrying the bottle with him, Jake wandered over to the balcony doors and stared out. Rain still pelted down. Below, cars glided along San Felipe Street, their lights reflecting red and white on the slick paving.

Well, he'd made his move. Soon, if he was careful and played this thing out right, he'd have his revenge. Jake's jaw clenched and his hand tightened around the glass bottle. Before he was through, Philip and Nathan were going to get a good dose of the same pain and humiliation they'd dealt out to the Taggarts.

Jake scowled. He was on the brink of fulfilling the promise he'd made to himself the day he left Zach's Corners. It was what he'd dreamed about, planned for, looked forward to. The thought of paying the Dushays back had kept him going during all those lean years.

So why wasn't he enjoying it more?

Jake took another sip of mineral water and sighed. Hell, he knew why. Because of Susannah.

She wasn't what he had expected. Dammit, she was a Dushay. She should have been spoiled and arrogant and too good for anything as common as work. Instead, right from the start she had surprised him. She was smart, industrious, eager to learn. Whatever task he assigned her, she applied herself to it without complaint—*and* she did a damned good job.

Even under trying conditions Susannah was pleasant and cooperative, and from what he'd observed, everyone else at Jetco liked her. No, she was neither arrogant nor self-centered. If anything, she struck him as being unsure of herself, even a bit on the shy side.

He thought about the kiss and her reaction to it, and a smile hovered about his mouth. Inexperienced, too. She'd been shocked right down to her toes. He'd be willing to bet that no man had ever kissed her that way before. It had scared her and shocked her but she'd enjoyed it, too. Almost as much as he had.

Jake frowned and took another swallow from the bottle. He hadn't expected that. If anything, when he'd settled on this plan, he'd been worried that he'd be repulsed by her—by who she was—and not be able to see it through. He sure as hell hadn't expected to like her.

He wished to hell he didn't. It would make things a lot easier. Jake swirled the remaining water, watching the liquid slosh up the sides of the green glass. Dammit! Why couldn't she be like the rest of the Dushays?

For the past week, all the while he'd been making his plans, deep down he'd had twinges of doubt about her, but he'd shoved them aside, refusing to accept that she wasn't like her father and half brother. After tonight, after seeing where she lived and learning what a rough deal life had dealt her and how she'd handled it, he couldn't keep ignoring the truth: Susannah was cut from a different bolt of cloth than Nathan and Philip.

When her parents had divorced, Susannah could have chosen to live with her father and enjoyed a life of luxury, but instead she'd remained with her mother. Not in his wildest dreams could Jake picture either Nathan or Philip living in such reduced circumstances if they had any other choice. Even less could he see either of them sacrificing their own life to care for an invalid, even if she was their mother or wife.

Thinking of Caroline Dushay reminded Jake of something that had bothered him earlier. He had been surprised to hear that she had left Nathan, but even more curious, was the timing of the divorce. The split must have occurred immediately after Jake had left Zach's Corners. Had Nathan's treatment of him and his family influenced Caroline's decision?

Jake had never given much thought to Caroline Dushay. Somewhere in the back of his mind he supposed he'd always assumed she was a shallow female who had married Nathan for his money and social position and had conveniently turned a blind eye to the man's less than honorable way of doing things. Now Jake wondered.

From what he'd seen of Susannah, she was a woman of character and integrity. Those weren't traits she had inherited from her father.

Hell, man. Just because you like the woman and feel sorry for her is no reason to start having doubts.

Jake tossed back the last of his drink and resisted the temptation to hurl the bottle across the room. Setting it down on the bar with a thump, he began to pace.

All right. There was no point in denying it; he had a bad case of conscience. But dammit! He had every right to strike back at Nathan. The bastard had ridden roughshod over other people for years with impunity. Not just the Taggarts. Nathan, and his father before him, had used every dirty trick, every low, underhanded scheme in the book to get where he was, without a thought to how much pain he inflicted or who he hurt. It was past time he got a little of his own back. And no one had more of a right to revenge than Jake and his family.

The trouble was . . . to even the score, he had to hurt Susannah.

Could he do it?

Jake's jaws clenched, making a muscle in his cheek jerk and twitch. His nostrils flared and whitened, and his eyes narrowed. He jerked to a halt and brought his fist down on the top of the bar with a force that rattled the decanters and made the empty bottle jump. "Yes, by heaven," he growled.

He wasn't going to go soft now. Everything he'd done, everything he'd worked for these past seventeen years—the struggle to get through college, the hand-to-mouth existence he'd endured, the scrabble to put his company together and make it pay, the risks he'd taken—had all been for one reason. The dream of retribution had been the driving force that had kept him going. He couldn't let a few pangs of conscience over one woman, particularly not Nathan Dushay's daughter, stand in his way. Besides, Susannah wasn't his problem.

Jake's mouth set in a grim line. It wasn't just Philip's treatment of Marianne. Perhaps if Nathan had been content to let it end there, Jake could have put the whole thing behind him.

His sister had been cruelly seduced by Philip's lies of undying love and promise of marriage, then abandoned, heartbroken and shamed, but that hadn't been enough for Nathan. He had wanted all trace of his son's indiscretion eliminated. Nathan had wanted no bastard grandchild growing up in Zach's Corners.

At nineteen, Jake had considered himself to be worldly wise and thoroughly cynical, but he'd never even seen it coming.

Naively, Jake had reported to work as usual the morning after his confrontation with Philip and Nathan. Lunch pail in hand, he had gotten in line with the other men to punch in, but when he'd reached the time clock, his card hadn't been in the rack.

"Hey, Taggart! Move it, will ya! You're holding up the line," someone behind him had hollered. "I ain't gonna git my pay docked on account of you. Now haul it!"

He shot the millhand a hard look and continued to search through the other time cards. When he couldn't find his, he cursed and strode inside in search of his foreman.

"Dammit, Owen, where the hell's my time card? I can't start work until I punch in, and some jerk in payroll goofed up and forgot to put it in the rack."

At the harsh demand, Owen McIntyre looked up from his clipboard. A look of regret entered his eyes when he spotted Jake. He sighed and ran a hand through his thinning gray hair. "I'm afraid there was no mistake, son. You've been let go."

Jake's head snapped back as though he'd received a blow. He stared at Owen, unable to believe what he'd heard. "You sure?"

"'Fraid so. Word came down first thing this morning from Mr. Dushay, himself. I'm real sorry, Jake. I like you, and you're a good worker. If it was up to me—"

"That bastard."

"Here now, Jake! Where're you going?" Owen hurried after him and caught his arm before he reached the stairs leading to the office. "Boy, are you crazy? You can't buck Nathan Dushay. Not in this town. He'll have your hide if you even try. He's the head honcho around here, boy, and there ain't nothing he likes better than proving it."

Owen looked up at the executive offices on the second level, where a soundproof glass wall overlooked the mill floor. Jake's gaze followed, and he stiffened. Nathan stood there like an arrogant overlord, feet spread wide, his hands on his hips, a taunting smile on his face, watching them.

"Easy, son," Owen cautioned. "Don't go doing anything foolish. It's what he wants. Can't you see that? Shoot, he'd have you arrested before you got to the top step, and what good would that do? Use your head, boy. Turn around and walk out."

Jake shot Owen a fierce glare, but the other man didn't even flinch. "I know it's hard, son, but just *do it.*"

Fury vibrated through Jake. He knew Owen was right. Still, common sense couldn't subdue the savage emotions roiling inside him.

Around the mill, awareness of the silent confrontation spread and, one by one, every hand stopped what he was doing to watch.

Jake stared at Nathan's arrogant smirk for a full minute, his body taut, the tendons in his neck standing out. He wanted, more than anything in the world, to storm up those steps and slam his fist into the man's face. Pride demanded it. Rage and frustration and primitive instinct egged him on. But through the morass of savage feelings, the faint voice of reason told him that to follow his instincts would only make his situation worse. Nathan Dushay had the power to make things rough on his family. Maybe even enough to have him sent to prison for assault. He'd do it, too. Even enjoy it.

"C'mon, son," Owen prodded in an urgent undertone. "Use your head for once instead of your fists. Walk away."

Owen was right. It galled Jake, but he knew he was right. Knowing, however, didn't make it any easier. It took every ounce of strength and will that Jake possessed to swallow his pride and fury, turn on his heel and walk out of the mill.

He felt sick inside, his gut churning. Staring straight ahead, he strode past the silent hands with his head high, his jaws and hands clenched, the rumble and whine of machinery roaring in his ears and the memory of Nathan's taunting smile burning into his soul.

He drove home like a bat out of hell, seeking release for his violent feelings in reckless speed, straining the engine in the dilapidated old truck to the limit.

Jake took the turn off the blacktop highway onto Tobin Road without reducing speed, slewing drunkenly close to the ditch on the opposite side, the truck's bald tires spinning in the loose dirt. Jake cursed and gunned the engine harder. The battered vehicle bounced and bucked down the corrugated road, fishtailing on sandy patches and kicking up a plume of boiling dust that trailed behind like a column of smoke. So black was Jake's mood, it was inconceivable to him that things could get worse.

Still seething, he brought his pickup to a jarring halt under the sweet gum tree before the leaning house. He slammed out, and behind him the engine sputtered and wheezed its last gasp as he stomped across the hard-packed dirt yard. Chickens scattered before him, clucking and squawking, their feathers ruffled. The old hound rose, stiff-legged, but his wagging tail slowed to a stop, and with a whine, he slunk away.

Jake leaped up onto the sagging porch. He reached for the door handle, but at the last second something caught his attention—a word, a flurry of movement within.... He stopped and peered in through the screen, and a sick feeling of apprehension seized his gut.

A clutter of boxes littered the floor of the front room. Jake watched his mother, who should have been working at the Culpepper house, moving about among them, stoically packing up their meager belongings while wiping away tears. Marianne was helping listlessly, her face devoid of all emotion.

In sharp contrast, Jake's father looked more animated and happy than he could remember ever seeing him. Will Taggart rushed about with a spring in his step, rubbing his hands together, his rummy eyes aglitter, offering hardy encouragement to the two women. Both ignored him.

"What the devil is going on here?" The screen door banged shut behind Jake as he came to an abrupt halt two steps inside the shabby living room and surveyed the jumble of boxes.

Leona Taggart looked up from packing wadded newspaper around a cheap ceramic lamp base. The desolation in his mother's eyes made Jake's heart leap. "We're moving, son." She struggled to control her wobbling chin. "Your dad has sold this place."

"What!" Jake whirled on his father.

Will took a hasty step back, his gleeful expression turning apprehensive.

"You sold this house? Why? No, don't tell me—for drinking money, right?"

"Now, son—"

"What I want to know is who the hell would buy this dump? And just what do you expect us to do for a place to live? Pitch a tent in the pasture?"

"We can't do that. Your father didn't just sell the house," his mother put in wearily without looking up from her labors. "He sold the land, too. All of it."

"What! You sold our land? Why you sorry—"

Will quailed before his son's wrath and backed away. His frightened gaze darted repeatedly to his wife, pleading for her support. "Now take it easy, son. That fifty acres wasn't doing us no good. There's not enough of it but to run a few head of cattle, and you know I ain't able to farm—"

"Don't give me that. The only thing wrong with you is a love for the bottle."

"Now, son, you ought not talk to your father that wa—"

"How much?"

"Huh?"

"How much did you get?"

"Well now, you know yourself that land in The Swamp ain't worth all that mu—"

"How much, damn you?"

"Five thousand."

"Five thousand. You sold all that was left of Great Grandpa Zachariah's land for a measly five thousand dollars?" Jake snarled. "Dammit, since I was twelve years old I've worked my butt off just to keep up the taxes on that land, and you practically give it away!"

"I didn't want to. Honest I didn't," Will insisted, but Jake knew from the avaricious glitter in his eyes that he was lying. Five thousand dollars was more money than his father had ever had at one time before in his life. "But what could I do? Mr. Dushay wouldn't go any higher."

"Dushay?" Jake forced the name out through clenched teeth, his voice vibrating with menace. "You sold our land to Nathan Dushay? You let him buy you off, didn't you? He wants the Taggarts out of Zach's Corners, doesn't he? Especially Marianne. So you took his lousy money and gave away our birthright. And for what? You'll drink it all up within a year."

Jake's hands opened and closed, over and over. A pulsing vein stood out in his temple and his nostrils flared with each furious breath. The urge to do violence pounded through him. Finally, with a roar of rage, he swung around and slammed his fist into the wall to keep from putting it through his father's face.

"Please, Jake, don't be too hard on him," Leona pleaded, placing her hand on his arm. He looked down into her red-rimmed eyes, and the pain he saw there tore at him. "Your father didn't have much choice. I no longer have a job—with the Dushays or any of the other families I cleaned for. Nathan saw to that. Just the same way he dismissed you. That attorney of his, Charles Goodwin, came by first thing this morning with the offer on the land and a message from Mr. Dushay that he wants us out of Zach's Corners immediately."

"Oh, he does, does he? Dammit! Just because Nathan Dushay snaps his fingers doesn't mean we have to jump," Jake raged. He turned on his father, radiating fury. "Why didn't you tell him to go to hell? Or were you too busy calculating how many bottles five thousand dollars would buy?"

"Jake," Leona pleaded. "Mr. Goodwin said we could either take the offer and leave, or Nathan would wait and buy up the place for back taxes when we failed to pay them. Then he would run us out of town.''

Jake opened his mouth to argue, but Leona stopped him with an upraised hand. ''Like it or not, that's exactly what would happen with neither of us working, and you know it.''

''We can get other jobs.''

''No. That's just the point, son. We can't.'' Leona sighed. Everything about her, the softness of her voice, her tired expression, her slumping shoulders, all cried defeat. ''You see, Mr. Goodwin made it quite plain that if we didn't leave, Nathan would see to it that no Taggart worked in this town—or even in this county—ever again.''

''That's right. So you see, son, I didn't have a choice,'' Will insisted.

Seething with frustration and fury, Jake exploded. ''You could have done *something!* Told him to take his offer and stick it in his ear! Thrown Goodwin out by the scruff of his neck!'' Jake paced to the other side of the room and swung back, raking his hand through his dark hair. ''Hell, I don't know. *Something!* Instead you knuckled under. The way you always do.''

''C'mon now, Jake,'' his father wheedled. ''Look on the bright side. With this much cash we can go someplace like Houston or Dallas, maybe start us up a little business. Who knows—this may turn out to be the best thing that ever happened to us. C'mon, whadda you say?''

''Start a business? With a measly five thousand?'' Jake snorted.

''Son, I know how you feel.'' His mother patted his arm and gazed at him sorrowfully. ''But what's done is done. We just have to make the best of it.''

''Maybe. But I'm not going anywhere with him,'' Jake snarled, casting a disgusted glance at his father. ''Neither are you or Marianne.''

Leona made a distressed sound, and Jake turned and grasped her shoulders, squeezing them urgently. "Mom, you know what will happen if you go with him. You'll watch him kill himself—little by little, day by day. Don't put yourself through that. He's not worth it. Come with me. The three of us—you, me and Marianne—we'll start over somewhere."

"Son, I'm sorry. I know you mean well, but...I...just can't." Leona cupped his cheek. Her palm was calloused and work-roughened, the skin red and chafed, but her touch was gentle. Her expression held love and sadness and resignation. "My place is with your father."

Her eyes glittered with moisture, and her voice quivered, but Jake could read the resolve in her face. He knew that she would not budge, no matter what he said.

Desperate, he turned to Marianne.

She sat in a tattered chair, staring vacantly at nothing. Jake knelt down before her and then took both her hands in his. "You'll come with me, won't you, sis? I'll take care of you and the baby. I'll go to college, get a good job. Things will be better for us then, you'll see. I swear it."

Marianne turned desolate eyes on him, and Jake's heart clenched. "What difference would it make where I go?" Her voice was a dull monotone, devoid of all feeling. "It wouldn't change anything that's happened."

"Mari—"

She placed her hand over his mouth, stopping the urgent plea. "No, Jake. I'll stay with Mom. You go ahead and do what you have to do. And later, if things work out as you plan, you can send for us."

Her apathy was as impossible to combat as their mother's determined loyalty. In the end Jake gave up and furiously stuffed his belongings into a paper sack, kissed his mother and sister goodbye and slammed out of the house without a word or a glance for his father.

To further exacerbate his dark mood, his battered pickup refused to start. Spitting out a vivid curse, Jake gave it a kick and marched up the dusty road with his sack of clothes under his arm and his jaw set. He didn't look back. When he reached the main highway he stood by the side and stuck out his thumb.

He had not been back to Zach's Corners since.

Savagely, Jake yanked off his necktie and tossed it aside. He sank down onto the sofa, sprawled on his spine, his long legs stretched out in front of him, his eyes narrowed. Even now, seventeen years later, thinking about what had happened brought back the same savage feelings, the same burning humiliation, the same sense of helpless frustration.

Only now he was no longer helpless. Now he had within his grasp a means of striking back. The time was right, and he was ready. His plans were set, and he'd made his preparations.

One of the smartest moves he'd made was sending Grant and Marianne to Europe. Grant was a great guy and a good friend, but Jake did not want to deal with his brother-in-law's disapproval just yet. Besides, he wouldn't put it past Grant to warn Susannah if he realized what was going on.

As it was, Jake had his work cut out for him.

From the first, something told him that Susannah would not be an easy conquest, and after talking to her tonight he was sure of it. She was as skittish as a young deer. He would have to proceed carefully. But no matter how long it took, she would eventually be his.

She's an innocent in all of this.

Jake frowned and shifted uneasily at the merciless prodding of his conscience. He surged to his feet and stalked back to the balcony doors. Dammit, Marianne had been an innocent, too. He couldn't let himself forget that.

Chapter Five

The following morning Susannah was profoundly grateful it was Saturday. After a horrible night spent tossing and turning, she slept late and awoke still tired and anxious, her eyes heavy-lidded.

To take her mind off Jake, and the thousand unanswered questions whirling in her head, she forced herself to do her normal Saturday chores. By late afternoon her weekly groceries were bought and put away, her laundry was done and the house was spotless, though no amount of cleaning could disguise its shabbiness.

Susannah plopped on the sagging sofa. She still needed to pay bills and balance her checkbook, but she was too tired to tackle another thing.

She took off her sneakers and put her head back, resting it against the high sofa back. Her eyes fluttered shut, and someone knocked on the front door.

Sighing, she heaved to her feet and trudged to answer the summons.

When she opened the door and stared up into Jake's piercing eyes every muscle in her exhausted body jerked to attention. Oh, no, she moaned silently. What was he doing there? She had counted on having the weekend to regain her equilibrium and shore up her defenses. He had caught her completely off guard. She didn't even have the consolation of looking halfway decent. She was, in fact, a mess.

Her hair was loose and hanging down her back in a wild cascade of curls; her jeans were so old they were almost white and they fit like a soft second skin; her sweatshirt, which had belonged to Marta's husband, hung halfway to her knees and clung to her body, no doubt clearly revealing that she was braless.

Jake's intent gaze skimmed over her, dropping down to her feet, clad in red wool socks, and drifting back up, lingering at her breasts in a way that had her fighting the urge to cross her arms protectively over her chest, then moving on, all the way up to her face, which bore not a speck of makeup.

"Are you going to invite me in?" It was more of an order than a question, his voice deep and commanding.

Susannah hesitated, then swallowed hard and moved aside without a word, and he stepped past her into the small, threadbare room. He was dressed more casually than she had ever seen him, in pleated slacks and a loose pullover sweater, but he still made her feel like something the cat had dragged home.

"Uh...won't you sit down," she invited, feeling awkward and nervous. With his imposing height and utter maleness, he seemed to overpower the small room. What was he doing here?

Jake sat down in the armchair, and Susannah perched on the edge of the sofa across from him and clasped her hands together. She groped for a topic of conversation but her mind went blank, and all she could do was wait for him to speak and pray he wouldn't notice how tense she was.

Jake noticed. He drew dark pleasure from her discomfort and deliberately prolonged it by remaining silent. Her fidgeting and the desperate panic in her soft green eyes revealed that she was aware of him, not as her boss, but as a man, and he liked that.

He tried to tell himself it was simply because her reaction boded well for his plan, but deep down he knew that the pleasure he derived from her response was more basic than that. He was attracted to her, and he wanted her to be attracted to him.

Her gaze met his and quickly skittered away. A smile tugged at Jake's mouth. At the same time he felt a rush of excitement. She reminded him of a young doe, fragile, frightened, unsure. Her edginess and the combination of beauty and vulnerability roused his predatory instincts. Suddenly, he wanted her. Quite fiercely.

He had caught her unawares, as he'd planned. Even so, her attire had surprised him. Despite what he'd learned, he was still having difficulty adjusting his perception of her. Even in these surroundings he had somehow expected to find her impeccably groomed, maybe wearing dressy slacks and a chic sweater and high heels, a strand of pearls at her neck, that cool, Dushay superiority firmly in place.

Instead, she looked adorably disheveled in those comfortable old clothes. Like an elegant waif. That, he realized suddenly, was exactly what she was. No amount of hard knocks or poverty or deprivation could destroy that innate aristocratic grace and manner. It was bred in the bone. Susannah could wear a feed sack with casual elegance and style . . . and make it look good.

From experience, he knew that most women looked pale and washed-out without their makeup. Susannah's face looked fresh and blooming, and years younger than the twenty-seven he knew her to be.

With relish, he surveyed her again, his gaze lingering on her breasts, and darkening as he realized their obvious freedom beneath the sweatshirt. Susannah blushed and squirmed, and desire surged through Jake.

The restless movement of her feet caught his eye, and his gaze dropped. A pink toe peeked through a hole in the sock on her left foot. A fresh tide of color spread over Susannah's cheeks, and she curled her toes under and put her right foot over her left. Jake grinned, finding both the tiny flaw and her reaction endearing . . . and somehow, sexy as hell.

"Have you thought about last night?" he asked abruptly.

Susannah stared at him, fighting down a bubble of hysterical laughter. As if she could think of anything else!

A verbal reply was beyond her; she could scarcely draw breath. Catching her bottom lip between her teeth, she nodded.

"I'm attracted to you, Susannah," he went on in that deep, rumbling voice. It slid over her skin like warm velvet. "Very attracted to you. As I believe I adequately demonstrated last night. I want to see you. Take you out."

Susannah looked away, unable to sustain that steady gaze any longer. "I . . . I don't think that would be a good idea."

"Why not? You're just as attracted to me as I am to you. You can't deny that, not after the way you responded when I kissed you."

Scalding heat flooded Susannah's entire body. She felt it radiating from her chest, neck and face in waves. Embarrassed almost to the point of tears, she squirmed on the sagging sofa cushion and kept her gaze averted. "I— It just wouldn't work." She gestured weakly with her hand. "We . . . we have to work together. And anyway, I thought you had a rule about not dating anyone employed by Jetco."

"There's an exception to every rule. For me, you're it."

With a sense of shock, he realized he had spoken the truth. He knew, suddenly, that even if she hadn't been Nathan's daughter, he would have pursued her. Rules be damned.

The admission shook him to the core, but not by so much as a flicker of an eyelid did Jake's expression change. He simply stared at her, his face dark and intent, his eyes glittering with deceptive lazy heat beneath half-lowered lids.

"No, really. It wouldn't . . . At the office . . . That is . . . it would make things too awkward. We couldn't—"

"We're both adults, Susannah," he said, cutting off her incoherent babble. "We can keep our private lives separate from our business relationship. When two people are so strongly attracted to one another as we are, it seems foolish to deny those feelings just because we happen to work together."

The desire Jake felt for Susannah disturbed him, but strangely, the more she resisted, the more he wanted her, and the more determined he became to overcome her objections. No matter what, Susannah was going to be his.

She dared to look at him then, cutting her eyes around and giving him a wary, sidelong look. Jake sucked in his breath and felt his loins grow heavy.

"Perhaps. But it still wouldn't work. I know it's not very sophisticated of me, but I don't think I could handle a casual relationship."

One of Jake's dark brows shot upward. "Did I, at any time, use the word 'casual'?"

Her face began to heat again, but Susannah forged on doggedly. "No, but . . . well . . . to be blunt, Mr. Taggart, I'm simply not interested in being one of a crowd. No offense intended, I assure you," she hurriedly tacked on. "It's just that . . . well . . . what with all the other women you date—"

"I've broken off with all of them."

"Wh-what?"

"That's what last week was all about. I took out each of the women I've been dating . . ." Pausing, Jake gave her a steady look, his mouth twitching ever so slightly. "Casually, I might add—and broke off with them so that I'd be free to pursue a relationship with you. And, by the way, my name is Jake. Use it."

Susannah stared at him. "La-last week? You mean you were planning this last week?"

"Susannah," he said patiently, as though talking to a child, "I knew from the very first that what was between us was serious. Very serious."

Stunned, Susannah could barely take it in. She had been sure that he didn't even like her, that all those times she'd caught him staring he'd been searching for and finding flaws. While she had been worrying that he might fire her and naively assuming that he was unaware of her as a woman, he'd been calmly and methodically planning to sweep her off her feet. She didn't know whether to feel flattered or angry. She experienced a little of both.

"You . . . you must have been very sure of me," she said, unable to keep the pique from her voice.

"Not at all. But I was sure of myself." Jake sat forward and swept her with a look that made her heart pound and did funny things to her stomach. "When I see something I want, I go after it, Susannah. And I don't give up until I get it. I learned a long time ago that success doesn't just happen. You make it happen. You work for it."

"I...I see." Susannah swallowed hard. "And...you want me."

"Yes. Very much."

The soft words made her heart rate double. She looked down at her hands, then looked back up, straight into those mesmerizing gray eyes that were watching her so steadily.

"I don't have affairs," she blurted out before she lost her nerve.

Jake didn't turn a hair. "I didn't think you did."

That stopped her cold. It wasn't at all the answer Susannah had expected. She blinked at him. "And . . . and you don't mind?'' she questioned in a voice riddled with disbelief.

"If you're asking if I want to make love to you, then the answer is yes. I want that very badly,'' he said with a candor that caused the bottom to drop out of her stomach. "On the other hand, if you're asking if I will push it, the answer is no.''

He stared at her, his gaze relentless and direct. "I want us to get to know one another, Susannah. To explore the possibilities open to us, see where they lead. But whatever happens, you can be sure I would never force you to do anything you didn't want to do. Remember that.''

The statement should have made Susannah feel better, but it didn't. She was very much afraid that this man could make her want what, if she were wise, she shouldn't.

Susannah wet her lips. He was offering her a chance to experience all of the things she had missed as a young girl: romance, excitement, courtship, the sharp, primitive pull of male to female, the sweet agony of perhaps falling in love. Part of her wanted to jump at what he was offering, but another part of her wanted to run from him, as far and as fast as she could. From the first, Jake Taggart had affected her that way; simultaneously she felt drawn to him and terrified of him. And she didn't know why.

Maybe it was the darkness she sensed below his controlled surface, that undercurrent of anger. There was no denying that he appealed to her, tempted her, more than any man she had ever met, but she sensed that Jake could hurt her. Badly.

"What, uh...what happens if things don't work out? Mother's medical bills were astronomical. I... really need my job.''

"Nothing that happens between us will affect your job at Jetco. Or, if you're uncomfortable with that, I can use my influence to get you another job elsewhere. But why go into a relationship assuming it's going to end?'' His gaze captured hers and delved deep, and Susannah felt a flutter in the region of her heart. "There is another possibility, you know."

With a shocking little thrill, she realized that he was talking about permanence, commitment, happy ever after. Susannah didn't want to think about that. She was having difficulty just dealing with the idea of dating him.

Common sense and an innate sense of self-preservation told her to tell him no. That was the cautious approach, perhaps the most sensible. But the raw, painful truth was, no matter the potential danger, she was irresistibly drawn to Jake... and, God help her, she wanted to be with him.

"Come on, Susannah," Jake coaxed, as though sensing her weakening. "Give me a chance. Give us a chance."

Gnawing her lower lip, she searched his face. Her heart fluttered in her chest like a wild thing. "All right," she whispered.

He sat there for a moment, unmoving, as though he were having difficulty absorbing her words. Then he smiled, slowly, a genuine smile that made his gray eyes crinkle. Susannah caught her breath. He wasn't handsome in the accepted sense, but on those rare occasions when Jake Taggart smiled, he could make a woman go weak in the knees.

"Good. Why don't I take you out to dinner? Do you like Mexican food?" At Susannah's nod he continued, not giving her a chance to decline. "Great. I know this little restaurant. It's nothing fancy but the food is out of this world. How soon can you be ready? I haven't eaten all day and I'm starving," he confessed.

Before Susannah could answer, a knock sounded on the front door and Marta stuck her head inside.

"Susannah, do you— Oh. Sorry. I didn't realize you had company."

Her friend's surprise was so obviously feigned that Susannah had to stifle a giggle. Marta was a born snoop and, where Susannah was concerned, a mother hen to boot. She had known perfectly well that Jake was there. His sports car was parked at the curb, after all, big as life. Marta had simply been unable to contain her curiosity a moment longer.

Marta studied Jake with unabashed interest, her lively hazel eyes taking in every detail. Knowing that her friend was bound to ferret out the reason for Jake's visit and what her reaction would be, Susannah made the introductions with the fatalistic air of one who has no choice.

"Jake has just invited me out to dinner," she added pointedly, biting the bullet and hoping that Marta would take the hint and leave. Susannah could have saved her breath.

Marta grinned. "Really? Well now, that's just great." She looked at Jake and added conspiratorially, "I keep telling this child it's high time she got out and enjoyed herself. You wouldn't believe how long she's been living like a nun, cooped up in this house with nobody but two old ladies for company."

Plopping her impressive girth down onto the sofa, Marta made a shooing motion at Susannah. "You just run along now. I'll keep your young man company while you get ready."

"Oh, but—"

"Go. Go," Marta commanded. "And don't worry about us. While you make yourself beautiful, Mr. Taggart and I will get acquainted."

That was precisely what Susannah was worried about. Give Marta ten minutes alone with him and she would have wormed out his life history, his political and religious affiliations, his net worth and his blood type. And Lord only knew what information Marta would give Jake about her.

"Marta—"

"Go on," Jake urged. "We'll be fine."

Left with no choice, Susannah darted a pained look between the two of them and reluctantly headed for the bedroom. At the door she swung back. "Oh! I'm forgetting my manners. Would you like something to drink, Mr. Ta—uh, Jake? I'm afraid all I can offer you is a soft drink, water or coffee. I don't have any spirits in the house."

"That's okay. I don't drink the hard stuff, anyway," Jake said, fighting back a grin at her transparent attempt to avoid leaving Marta alone with him.

"Oh...well...then I, uh..." Susannah waved her hand vaguely toward the rear of the duplex. "I guess I'd better go, uh . . . get cleaned up. Excuse me."

Jake watched her pad across the threadbare rug in her red socks, his gaze on the gentle sway of her hips beneath the enveloping sweatshirt. The night before he had held that firm flesh in his hands, pressed her tightly against him, felt her quivering response. He wanted to do it again. The thought of arousing her to passion interfered with his breathing and sent heat straight to his loins.

He hadn't realized how much he'd wanted her to accept his suit. When she'd hesitated, he'd experienced several seconds of sheer panic. He'd known that he could eventually wear her down, steamroll over her objections with sheer persistence, but somehow it had become vital to him, in a way that he didn't want to probe too deeply, that she accept him freely.

Susannah disappeared into the bedroom, and Jake turned to find Marta watching him.

"So, you're Susannah's new boss. I've been hoping I'd get to meet you. She has told me a lot about you."

"Has she?" Jake smiled, inordinately pleased.

Marta did not respond to Jake's hard-edged charm as most women did. Instead she treated him to the same probing scrutiny that he used on others, her steady gaze stabbing deep, as though she were studying the secrets of his soul. "I think the world of that girl," she announced without so much as blinking. "My late husband, Harry—God rest his soul—and I were never blessed with children, but that little gal, why, she's just like a daughter to me."

Jake nearly laughed aloud, something he did all too rarely. You couldn't miss the not-so-subtle warning in Marta's words and pointed stare.

He studied her curiously, amazed that Susannah had formed a bond with the frowsy woman. They were as opposite as any two females could be. Marta, with her wild, dyed red hair and overdone makeup, her stout body draped in some sort of ridiculous flowing garment, baubles and bangles hung all over her, clanking every time she moved, looked like a poor imitation of a gypsy, and the antithesis of refinement and class. Nathan and Philip would not have deigned to speak to a woman like Marta.

"Tell me, Mr. Taggart, when is your birthday?"

Jake's heavy eyebrows shot skyward at the abrupt change of subject. "November fourteenth. Why?"

"Perfect. Just as I thought. And I'll bet you started that company of yours yourself, didn't you? Probably on a shoestring."

"Yes. As a matter of fact, I did. How did you know?"

"Because you're a Scorpio. All you Scorpios have within you the power to rise from the ashes of defeat like a phoenix and soar to great heights," she explained with a dramatic wave of her arm that set the chiffon drapery to fluttering and clanged the row of bracelets dangling from her wrist. "For that reason, many Scorpios are self-made men."

"Ahh, I see. You're referring to astrology." Jake's mouth twitched, and a hint of disdain glittered in his eyes.

"Yes. And you can wipe that look off your face, young man. I won't tolerate any disrespect from a young whippersnapper like you," Marta snapped, surprising Jake into obedience.

It had been years since anyone had dared to reprimand him. *Or* since he'd been referred to as young. He grinned suddenly, a genuine display of mirth crinkling the corners of his eyes. Darned if she didn't remind him of his mother. Not in looks, but certainly in attitude. Leona Taggart had been the essence of kindness but she had drilled good manners into her children and hadn't hesitated to box their ears when they failed to use them. Without her knowing it, Marta's stock with Jake took a quantum leap skyward.

All trace of scorn and cool reserve vanished from his face. "Yes, ma'am. You're right, of course. I apologize."

"Well, that's better. Whether you believe it or not, astrology is a very useful tool. It can be a guide in making important decisions. Things like when to invest your money and in what, the best time for travel, what kind of profession you're best suited to. What woman is best for you." The last was tacked as though it were an afterthought, but he caught the quick look she gave him out of the corner of her eye.

"Is that right?" Jake responded, suppressing a grin.

"Oh, absolutely. For instance, Susannah is a Pisces and her chart recently indicated that she would meet a Scorpio, one who would have a dramatic impact on her life."

"Oh, really?"

"Yes." Marta's eyes narrowed on his expressionless face. "*Are* you going to have an impact on her life, Mr. Taggart?"

Jake felt a twinge of unease. He didn't believe in that astrology hocus-pocus, but he did belive that Marta was a very intuitive woman. It wouldn't do to have her as an enemy. Frankness, where possible, he decided, was the best course. "Yes, Marta," he said, looking her right in the eye. "I do believe I am."

She held his gaze for several seconds, then sighed and relaxed. "Good. That child needs a strong man to care for her. And a Scorpio is perfect—provided his darker side is kept under control." Marta scowled and pointed a finger at him. "And don't think for a moment that I don't know about that darker side of yours, Mr. Taggart. All Scorpios have one. You just see to it that yours doesn't affect Susannah."

"Yes, ma'am," Jake said, hiding his guilt and discomfort behind a blandly amused look.

Pleased with his response, Marta smiled. She fiddled needlessly with the folds of chiffon covering her lap and gave him a quick, guileless look. "Pisces is very compatible with Scorpio, you know."

Jake grinned. He couldn't help it.

Susannah hurried through her shower and dressed in record time. She emerged from the bedroom to find Marta and Jake talking together as though they'd been close friends for years. A more incongruous pair she would have been hard-pressed to imagine than the tough, urbane man and her unconventional landlady, but they seemed to be getting along famously.

Because Jake was so hungry, they left for the restaurant at once. Susannah sat across from him, chewing the spicy food in a daze, so bemused and enthralled she was barely aware of the times she bit into a jalopeño pepper.

It seemed unreal to her that she, who had, until now, had exactly five dates, four of which had been with pimply faced teenagers, was sitting there with Jake Taggart. He was a man over whom every female at Jetco under the age of fifty drooled, a man who was the epitome of every romantic daydream Susannah had ever had, a man who oozed sex and danger as easily as other men did sweat. Susannah felt woefully out of her league... and excited beyond words.

They talked of numerous things—politics, movies, Houston's abominable weather. Or at least, Jake did. Susannah mostly listened. She felt painfully shy and unsure of herself. As she watched those sculpted lips move, and let the deep, rumbling tones pour over her, it seemed a dream. It was all so ordinary, so calm that she could almost believe that those fevered moments in his arms the night before had not occurred. Almost.

Those years when Susannah had worked at home she had met quite a few men—graduate students, businessmen, ministers who needed their sermons typed. Once, even a truck driver who was taking a correspondence course. When they had come to pick up the work she'd done for them, more than one had hung around to talk, and she had known they were interested in her as a woman. She had enjoyed the attention and the conversation, but none had ever roused more than a vague curiosity. Toward most she felt indifferent.

She was not indifferent to Jake. She felt alive, on edge, her skin tingly, as though every nerve ending were raw and exposed. She tried to hide her vulnerability behind a rapt expression and a polite smile, but she had a suspicion that Jake saw right through her, and that he was pleased by her quivering response.

Jake concentrated on Susannah with an intensity that she found flattering, and a bit unsettling. His vivid gaze rarely left her face. He drew her out about her mother, asking gentle questions, making gentle comments. He asked about her family, about Marta, about the kind of life she'd led up until now. He was charming her with his rumbling, honeyed voice and his direct, beguiling eyes, and Susannah didn't care.

Inevitably the conversation turned to business, and Susannah began to relax. She had learned enough about the computer business to contribute to the conversation, if only in a minor way.

She found the story of how Jake had hocked almost everything he'd owned and borrowed to the hilt to start the company, and his first years of struggle and holding off creditors, utterly fascinating.

She wasn't at all surprised that he had succeeded. Jake was a brilliant business strategist. Susannah felt that it had probably been inevitable that he would end up occupying a position of authority, whether at the helm of his own company or working for someone else. Jake had the forceful personality, the intelligence and the determination to reach the top, no matter what he tried.

They talked about a multitude of things, but the one thing they didn't talk about was Jake's family, not even his sister, whom Susannah knew was married to Grant. Whenever she inquired about her or anything prior to the time he started college he adroitly shifted the focus elsewhere, and after a while she realized that the subject was forbidden territory and avoided it, though deep down she was curious.

On the ride home Susannah fell silent once again. Whatever small amount of tenseness she had shed during the past few hours came rushing back as they neared the run-down duplex. Several times she felt Jake's glance rake over her, but she clasped her hands together and stared straight ahead.

Susannah's heart boomed as Jake walked her to the door, her pulse reverberating in her ears. The draperies on Marta's side of the house twitched, and she wondered if Jake had noticed. She felt like a sixteen-year-old coming home from her first date.

She unlocked the door and reached inside, groping along the wall for the light switch and flipping it on before turning back to face Jake. "Well...good night. Thank you for a nice evening." It had been more than nice. It had been wonderful. The stuff dreams were made of, for all its ordinariness. Her dreams, at any rate.

"Good night," Jake said, but he didn't move. He simply stood there, regarding her intently. The porch light was tactfully off, and there was only the moon glow to provide light. It washed out all colors and left only the darkness of his hair and eyes and the pale sheen of her silvery curls forming a halo around her head and shoulders.

He lifted his hand and captured a curl. It coiled around his finger as though it had a life of its own, pale writhing silver against dark skin. Something flared in Jake's eyes, and Susannah felt her heart kick into a higher gear.

Releasing the lock, Jake ran the back of his knuckles down her cheek, and his eyelids drooped as though they had suddenly grown heavy. He cupped her jaw and brushed the pad of his thumb over her soft lips. His hand curved around her neck, his fingers invading the mane of curls that frothed around her nape, drawing her to him. He bent his head, and Susannah went weak with anticipation, her body a mass of quivering nerves and fevered longing.

He was going to kiss her again. This, she realized, was what she'd been waiting for all night.

His mouth brushed hers, once, twice. He raised his head and looked into her wide eyes, then kissed her again, slanting his mouth over her parted lips with a tenderness that stole her breath away.

Susannah sighed and melted against him.

It was all the encouragement Jake needed. His arms came around her, sure and strong, pulling her tightly against his chest, deepening the kiss, but going slow, giving her all the time in the world to reject him. The thought never occurred to Susannah.

Her love-starved heart craved this. She had been without human touch, human warmth for so long. So long. She had never known the hungry wanting of a man, the sweet quickening response his aggressive demand sparked, the thrill of passion swelling and building until it was a delicious ache.

She felt his heat burning her through the layers of clothing. That warmth drew her like a magnet. She went up on tiptoe and wound her arms around his neck, pulling him closer, eagerly accepting the intimate intrusion of his tongue. A raw, naked yearning began building inside her. She strained against him, wanted to get closer, to gather him in until his flesh was hers, and hers was his.

She kissed him with all the pent-up hunger and need of a lifetime, too lost in the pleasure of it all to worry that she might be giving him the wrong impression, that he might arrive at the conclusion that she was a woman who, despite her earlier claim, indulged her sexual appetite freely. In truth, Susannah wasn't sure, at that moment, if she could resist Jake, should he pick her up and carry her inside to her bedroom . . . or if she even wanted to.

But it was Jake who ended the kiss, though she felt the fine tremor that ran through him when he tucked her head against his shoulder and laid his cheek against her crown. For a moment he simply held her, letting the storm of passion subside. Then he reached up and gently disentangled her arms, giving her a wry look as he steadied her and stepped back. "If I don't stop now I won't be able to." He leaned down and brushed another kiss against her lips. "Good night, sweetheart. I'll call you tomorrow."

Susannah stared at him, dazed and not quite steady on her feet. She ached. Her body felt abused, betrayed, but she knew he was right; they had to stop. Thank goodness Jake had had the strength to do so; she wasn't at all certain that she could have.

"Good night," she whispered, and slipped inside.

She leaned back against the door and put her hand over her mouth. Her lips were still wet from his kiss, tender and puffy. From outside came the sound of his car starting, the subdued growl of the powerful engine as he drove away.

Susannah closed her eyes. Her chest rose and fell with each deep breath. Terror and longing engulfed her. In her heart she knew that she was on the brink of falling in love. Teetering on the edge. Being pulled over the precipice. All it would take to send her toppling was a tiny push.

Chapter Six

The first nudge came on Monday morning. Susannah arrived at work feeling blue and hurt. All day Sunday she had waited by the phone, falling on it with the avidity of a starving man at a banquet every time it rang, but Jake had not called as he'd promised. By the time she went to bed she was berating herself for swallowing his line and calling herself all manner of fool.

That hadn't stopped her from tossing and turning half the night or from experiencing a hollowness in the pit of her stomach the next morning. She felt so stupid, so gullible. She hadn't wanted to face Jake, and had actually toyed with the idea of calling in sick ... even of calling in her resignation. Luckily, her common sense had taken over, reminding her just how much she needed her job.

Nevertheless, when she walked into the office that she shared with Alice, a heavy feeling of dread pressed in on her chest like a stone.

"Good morning. What's your favorite color?" Alice asked before Susannah reached her desk.

Accustomed to Marta's mysterious babbling, Susannah barely paid any attention. "I don't know. Green, I guess. Or maybe a dusty rose." She dropped her purse in the bottom drawer of her desk and sat down with a sigh, her shoulders drooping.

"Green it is. I don't think they offer dusty rose. So how about a dark metallic? They have one called Mystic Nile."

"What?" Glancing at Alice, Susannah saw that she was pouring over a pile of brochures. "What are you talking about?"

"The color car you want. Jake called this morning from California—"

Susannah's head snapped up. "Jake's in California?"

"Uh-huh. He had to make a rush trip out there yesterday. There was an explosion and fire at the plant we're building and a man was injured. Jake called just a few minutes ago. Evidently, he's been at the hospital with the man's wife for the past twenty-four hours."

Susannah wondered if he'd asked to speak to her, but she didn't dare inquire; Alice was too shrewd for Susannah to risk it. Instead she sat there, feeling guilty and happy and weak with relief.

"He said for both of us to pick out the make, model and color car we want and go ahead and order them, in case he doesn't get back for a few days. I'm going for a sporty model. How about you?"

Susannah was so lost in her happy daze it took a few seconds for Alice's words to sink in. When they did, she frowned. "Did you say car? What car?"

"The one you're getting."

"But I'm not buying a car. I can't afford one."

"You can this one. It'll be a company car. Jake's buying."

"He can't do that!"

"Sure he can. He's the boss."

"But we can't let him. It isn't right. It's—"

"Look, Susannah, don't look a gift horse in the mouth, okay. I, for one, am looking forward to tooling around in this little red job," Alice said, tapping a brochure with one perfectly manicured nail. "Besides, why should you care if Jake adds two more company cars to his fleet?"

Susannah opened her mouth, then closed it. There was simply no way she could explain her objection. She couldn't tell Alice that Jake was buying the cars because of her, because they were sort of... well... about to become involved. Maybe.

Jake didn't want her riding the bus anymore, or getting home late and walking those dark streets, she realized suddenly and experienced a warm rush of emotion. Susannah stared off into space, a soft smile on her face. He was trying to disguise his motive by providing Alice with a car, as well, but Susannah knew what he was up to.

It was a sweet thing for him to try to do, but of course, she couldn't let him buy her a car.

She knew better than to say so to Alice, however, so she hemmed and hawed over which one to choose. Finally she instructed Alice to go ahead and make her own selection as she still wanted to think about hers. As soon as Jake returned, Susannah intended to explain to him that she couldn't possibly accept his generous offer.

Still, all day long, whenever Susannah thought about the incredibly thoughtful gesture, she got a warm feeling... and felt herself being drawn closer to the brink.

The opportunity to confront Jake came quicker than Susannah expected. A little after five that evening she was standing at the bus stop in front of the building with ten or fifteen other Jetco employees when a sleek silver Porsche braked to a stop at the curb in front of them. Excitement, then panic, fluttered through Susannah. It couldn't be.... He wouldn't....

It was, and he did.

The passenger door opened, and Jake leaned across the seat, his gray eyes homing in on Susannah. He smiled, a slow, hard, sexy smile that shut down her breathing. "Get in," he said in that soft rumble.

Several of the women gasped and looked at Susannah in astonishment. She tried to ignore them, *and* the fiery blush climbing her neck.

"Why, uh…thank you, Mr. Taggart. It's kind of you to offer me a ride, but there's no need. Really. The bus will be here any second," she said in an ultrapolite voice, begging him with her eyes not to do this.

Jake ignored her silent plea. "Get in, Susannah," he insisted in that same soft tone. "Or I'll get out and put you in. Which will it be?"

With the rapt attention of Wimbledon spectators, the wide-eyed gazes of their audience swept back and forth between Jake and Susannah. Left with no choice and blushing hotly, Susannah hurriedly slipped into the car.

For a few seconds they just sat there, and Susannah stared straight ahead, terrified that he might take it into his head to kiss her, right there in front of everyone. From the way he was looking at her she knew that he'd given the idea some thought, but finally he shifted gears and they pulled away from the curb.

"Why did you do that?"

"Do what? And don't I even get a hello?"

"Why did you pick me up? Now everyone will think we're involved."

"Susannah, we *are* involved."

"But no one was supposed to know. You said— Oh! *Oh!*"

Jake hit the brakes and swerved, throwing Susannah forward against her seat belt and bringing the car to an abrupt halt at the curb. Before she could do more than bounce back against the padded seat, he unlatched both his safety belt and hers, twisted around and hauled her up against him.

"Jake, wh—"

His mouth cut off her startled cry, slanting over hers hungrily. With quick, sure strokes, his tongue thrust into her mouth over and over, telling her of his impatient need.

Susannah went utterly still, frozen with shock. Then the slow curl of heat started low in her belly, and she shivered and melted against him. They could have been standing in the middle of Main Street in the rush-hour traffic for all she knew... or cared. When Jake kissed her that way, every thought flitted right out of her mind. All she could do was feel, and marvel at the searing pleasure he could bestow with just his hard mouth and strong, possessive hands.

The blast of a horn broke the spell. Jake raised his head and looked at her, but he continued to hold her close. His smile was wry, but passion still darkened his eyes.

"What I said was, we would keep our business and private lives separate, not secret. There's no way we can hide our relationship from others. I don't even want to. I'm not about to watch everything I say and do. If I feel like touching you or kissing you, I'm damned well going to."

She stared at him, both thrilled and appalled by his fierce possessiveness. Things were moving too quickly. She couldn't think straight. Especially when he was holding her like he was. "Jake, I—"

"Shh." He brushed her mouth with another kiss, and Susannah forgot what she was about to say. When he raised his head, she trembled and curled into him with a sigh.

A low chuckle rumbled from Jake, and with a slight, hard smile that reeked with masculine triumph, he put her back in her seat, fastened the seat belts and put the car into gear.

Susannah settled back against the buttery leather with a dreamy smile on her face and stared at Jake's profile through slitted eyes. She felt as happy and content as a lazy cat in the sunshine. She could almost purr.

"So. Did you order your car?" Jake asked, checking the traffic in the rearview mirror. He flipped down the turn signal and eased into the next lane.

"The car!" Susannah bolted to attention, the sweet lethargy vanishing instantly. "No, I certainly did not. Jake, I can't accept a car from you."

He scowled and sent her a sharp look. "Why not?"

"Because... well... it just wouldn't be right."

"What's wrong with buying company cars for my employees?"

"Oh, come on, Jake. We both know why you're doing this," Susannah scolded gently. "You're concerned because I don't have a car. I know how you feel about me riding the bus and walking home from the bus stop late at night."

"You're wrong. It so happens that I'm concerned about Alice and Pete. What with his medical bills and having to take early retirement, things are bound to be tight financially, but Alice would never complain or ask for help." He shrugged. "I'm just trying to make things a little easier for them."

Susannah studied him for several seconds through narrowed eyes. "I don't believe you. You just made that up."

"Oh, yeah?" Jake smiled. "Prove it."

Nonplussed, Susannah could only continue to stare. How on earth did you fight a determined man like Jake?

The answer was obvious: you didn't. Even if she won this argument he would find another way to make her take the car. That strong-willed, "never say die" streak was as much a part of Jake as his black hair and gray eyes. So was that awesome power and intensity that ran just beneath his calm surface. They were the qualities that had allowed him to build his company from scratch and kept him on top in the cutthroat world of big business. Everything Jake wanted in life he went after with the same single-minded determination…herself included, Susannah realized with a tiny sense of shock.

It occurred to her that once committed to a course of action, nothing and no one could deter him; right or wrong, Jake would always see a thing through to the bitter end.

Which was fine if you were on his side, but heaven help the poor wretch who incurred his wrath.

The thought came out of nowhere and, inexplicably, Susannah felt a chill of alarm trickle down her spine.

Glancing her way, Jake saw her worried expression and sighed. "Look, Susannah, just accept the car as one of the perks of your job and let's drop the subject. Okay? I'm too beat to argue about it. Except for catnaps, I haven't slept in thirty-six hours or eaten in twelve, and that's only if you count that cardboard stuff that comes out of a vending machine."

Susannah was immediately stricken with guilt. For the first time since getting into the car she noticed the signs of exhaustion about Jake. Whisker stubble shadowed his jaw, and beneath his bloodshot eyes there were dark circles. Weariness and worry had deepened the lines bracketing his mouth and gave his skin a gray cast beneath his tan. His shirt was wrinkled, the top three buttons undone, his missing necktie stuffed into the pocket of his suit coat. His hair was mussed, as though he'd combed his fingers through it repeatedly. He looked haggard and disheveled and utterly drained, and Susannah felt wretched and selfish for not noticing sooner.

"Oh, Jake. I'm so sorry. I completely forgot about the accident. How is the man who was injured?"

"He's stable now, but it was touch and go for a while. I stayed at the hospital with his wife until they took him off the critical list. Then I spent today at the construction site. The damage is extensive, but insurance should cover it." He cupped his hand around the back of his neck and absently massaged tired muscles. The gesture tugged at Susannah's heart.

"You should be home in bed," she scolded softly.

Jake turned his head and seared her with a long, hot look. *Yes. With you.*

Had he spelled it out in neon lights, he could not have made the thought clearer.

Susannah felt a rush of desire so strong it made her weak. She stared back, and shuddered helplessly.

When he was in town and didn't have a business dinner scheduled, Jake took her out every night. He was rushing her shamelessly, doing his best to sweep her off her feet. Susannah was flattered, and at the same time alarmed.

To Susannah, the whole thing had a dreamlike quality to it. Her dull, ordinary life had suddenly changed to a fantasy come true. Jake took her places she had never been, showered her with attention, and aroused in her a passion she had never known she possessed. With a look, a simple touch, he could render her breathless. When he kissed and caressed her, which he did often, she lost all sense of time and place.

Susannah laughed when she remembered how, at their first meeting, she had thought him cold. He was anything but. For all his outward control, underneath, Jake sizzled. He was an ardent, sensual man with a tough, tender way about him that sent a thrill right to her feminine core.

On one level, Susannah was deliriously happy. She enjoyed to the fullest every moment she had with Jake. But some innate sense of caution caused her to hold back.

When he kissed her good-night, he lingered over it, the caress light and leisurely, but the tentative nibbles always escalated into passion, and soon they would be locked in each other's arms, kissing with the pent-up fervor of randy teenagers.

Susannah knew that Jake wanted more. For that matter, her own body clamored for release from the sweet pain his nearness produced. But, true to his word, Jake did not pressure her, and she always drew away before any deeper intimacy developed between them.

At first Susannah wasn't sure exactly why. Perhaps, she mused, because it all seemed too good to be true. Or perhaps because Jake's intensity still made her nervous. Or perhaps she was afraid of being dominated, of losing her identity, her sense of self, to an overpowering man like Jake.

All of those things were true, but they did not really concern Susannah; they were merely excuses, she finally admitted to herself. What held her back was simply her fear of loving the wrong man. Always, hovering somewhere in the back of Susannah's mind was the memory of her mother's tragic love for her father.

Cold and conniving though Nathan Dushay was, it wasn't difficult for Susannah to understand why Caroline had fallen in love with him. When Nathan chose, he could be utterly charming and gallant, especially around an attractive woman. That was the man her mother had loved. Susannah suspected that, even though Caroline could not accept his faults or his ruthless treatment of others, she had loved him to the end. With her last breath, she had whispered his name.

And he had not even bothered to attend her funeral.

The thought of making the same sort of mistake terrified Susannah. So she held back and tried desperately not to love Jake, but with every day that passed, the more she learned about this intense, complicated man, the more she teetered over the edge of the precipice. She knew if she ever took that fall, it would be forever.

True to his word, Jake never truly tried to seduce her. He never even took her to his apartment. Perversely, she was a bit hurt by the omission, until he happened to mention that his teenaged nephew was staying with him until school was out and he could join his parents in Europe. Susannah realized then that Jake was merely being circumspect because of the boy, and she admired him all the more for it.

Jake had no trouble keeping their personal and business relationships separate, as Susannah had feared would be the case. That fact was amply demonstrated one afternoon, a few weeks after Jake's return from California, when a scruffy old man walked in unannounced.

He was dressed in patched and faded overalls and a battered straw hat. Except for being clean, he looked like he'd just come in from working in the fields all day.

Susannah cast a quick look around, but Alice was not to be seen. "May I help you, sir?" she inquired politely.

"No, ma'am. Don't trouble yourself. I've just come to see Jake, is all," he said, heading toward the inner office.

"Sir, wait!" Susannah jumped up and flew around the desk like a shot, intercepting him before he reached the door. "You can't go in there." Jake would have her head if she let this man disturb him.

"But I gotta—"

"Do you have an appointment?" she asked, knowing perfectly well that he hadn't. At that moment Jake was consulting with Harve Freeman, the company's chief attorney, and he had a meeting with his regional managers after that.

The old man began to look worried. He took off his straw hat and turned it around and around in his huge hands, casting desperate looks at Jake's door. "No, ma'am, I ain't got no appointment, but I always—"

"I'm sorry, sir. But no one gets in to see Mr. Taggart without an appointment." Touching the man's elbow, Susannah urged him toward the outer office. "Why don't you talk to the secretary outside? She can tell you when Mr. Taggart might be able to see you."

"Miss Dushay! What do you think you're doing?"

The barked question made Susannah jump. She spun around and found herself facing Jake's hard stare. In those piercing eyes was no sign of the man who had kissed her senseless only the night before. "Why...I...I was just—"

"Elvie is an old friend of mine. He doesn't need an appointment to see me. Ever."

"Ye-yes, sir. I'm sorry. I...I didn't know."

Avoiding her eyes, Harve Freeman mumbled a quick "excuse me," skirted around them and scooted out the door, passing Alice on her way in.

"That's right, Jacob. She didn't," Alice said, dumping a stack of bifold printouts onto her desk. "So don't get on Susannah's case."

She gave Jake a meaningful look, then smiled at the old man. "Hello, Elvie. It's good to see you. How's it going?"

"Not too good, Alice. Not too good. That's why I come to see Jake, here."

"Come on, Elvie, we'll talk inside," Jake said, and ushered the man into his office.

Susannah's bewildered gaze sought Alice's. "Who is that?"

"That's Elvie Peterson. He and his wife, Fayrene, are old friends of Jake's. Last year a paint manufacturer built a facility on land adjacent to their farm. Within six months traces of toxic chemicals began showing up in soil samples from Elvie's fields, and now all of his water wells are contaminated. Jake is helping them bring suit against the paint manufacturer and giving them a hand financially, until the case is settled."

"Really?"

Alice chuckled. "Don't look so stunned. Jake may seem remote and hard, but he's a loyal friend. Elvie and Fayrene's place is just outside of College Station. Back when Jake was working his way through A & M University they provided him with room and board in exchange for a few chores around the place."

"That was very nice of them, I'm sure, but still . . . to go out on a limb like that for someone seems like an extraordinary thing to do."

Alice shrugged. "Jake never forgets a favor. Of course, on the other hand, he never forgets an injury, either."

The statement was so similar to something Marta had said that Susannah started. "Wh-what?"

"That's just the way Jake is. If you befriend him, there's nothing he won't do for you. Shoot, I could name a whole list of people who have benefited from his loyalty."

Susannah glanced at the closed door of Jake's office, and her gaze softened. "Really?"

Alice frowned at her sappy look. "Yes, really. But before you go fitting him for a halo, bear in mind that those who've slighted him or done him dirty have felt the scorpion's sting, much to their regret."

Susannah heard her, but it was too late. She had already stepped off the cliff.

During her saner moments, usually those solitary times when Jake wasn't around, Susannah was appalled that she had let herself fall in love with him. He was not at all the kind of man she had envisioned herself spending her life with. She had dreamed of someone kind and gentle, someone ordinary. Not a tough, complex, driven man like Jake Taggart. Always assuming that Jake even wanted to get married. He was attracted to her and he wanted her, but even she wasn't inexperienced enough to believe that was anything but lust. He had certainly never, by word or action, given her any reason to believe that he loved her. Oh, Lord, Susannah. What have you done? she asked herself countless times in the middle of the night. What have you done?

Jake and Susannah had been dating a little over two months when she finally met Pierce Sorrenson, the banker who was financing Jetco's expansion. Until then he had merely been a voice over the telephone, but when he came strolling into the office, Susannah understood why the mention of his name created such a flurry among the females in the company.

Pierce Sorrenson did not fit Susannah's idea of a stuffy banker at all. He was a tall, lean, southern aristocrat with a honeyed Virginia drawl, a shock of chestnut hair and the wickedest blue eyes that Susannah had ever seen. He wasn't just handsome; he was devastating. He had about him a classic, ageless male beauty and indefinable style that set female hearts of all ages aflutter. Even hopelessly in love with Jake as she was, Susannah was not completely immune. When he turned those wicked eyes and the full force of his charm on her, she felt a giddy rush of pleasure, her face blooming with color.

He wasted no time. The minute Pierce strolled into the office and spotted her, he made a beeline for her desk, introduced himself and asked her out to dinner.

Flustered, Susannah could only stare at him for a moment. Before she found her tongue, Jake appeared in the doorway to his office and snapped, "Knock it off, Sorrenson. I didn't ask you over here so you could hit on my assistant."

Pierce gave Jake a disgusted look and shuddered. "What a truly vulgar expression. That was not 'hitting on,' you uncouth lout. That was the opening gambit of a rite of courtship." He winked at Susannah and touched her hot cheek with his forefinger. "Pay no attention to that barbarian. The man has no poetry in his soul. We'll continue this later," he added with a wink.

Not one whit intimidated by Jake's glower, Pierce strolled toward him with an urbane smile on his handsome face. "Crass millhand," he muttered with the easy familiarity of long friendship as he passed Jake and stepped into the inner office.

Jake paused long enough to give Susannah a searching look. Something in his unsmiling face caused her heart to lurch, then start to pound so hard her chest hurt. Finally, without a word, he stepped into his office and closed the door with a soft click.

Jake leaned back in his desk chair and solemnly studied his old friend. Pierce was a devil with the ladies. He had a reputation to uphold and he flirted with every pretty female as a matter of course. Still . . . Jake didn't like the way he'd looked at Susannah.

"Stay away from her."

The blunt order sent Pierce's eyebrows skyward. "I presume we're talking about the delectable creature in the outer office?" At Jake's nod, Pierce looked at him sharply, then sighed. "Ahh, I see. You've beaten me to her, haven't you?"

"I'm her employer," Jake hedged. "I feel responsible for her."

That drew a snort from Pierce. "Oh, come on, man. I employ dozens of women but I don't watch over them as though they were my sisters. You've even dated some of them. Hell, you've dated my sister, come to think of it."

Jake chuckled, and felt the coil of tension in his stomach loosen. It was difficult to be annoyed with Pierce. Just as using the oblique approach with him was pointless. He was always unfailingly cheerful, and as direct as a poke in the eye. Which was one of the reasons Jake liked him. Pierce might make a play for Susannah, but he'd do it openly and laugh if you objected.

"True. But I still want you to stay away from Susannah."

"Are you sure you're speaking as her boss? Or is your objection personal?"

"Both."

"I see," Pierce said with a despondent sigh. "Tell me. Is it serious?"

"Yes."

"As in marriage?"

Jake started. "Hardly." Good Lord! He had never even considered marrying Susannah. Merely thinking about it gave him a funny feeling.

But that didn't mean he was willing to let Pierce have a shot at her. And it wasn't just because of his plan, either, he admitted reluctantly. He'd been wooing her with excruciating care, proceeding slowly so as not to spook her. He'd gotten past her initial fear of him. Now she trembled sweetly in his arms, her exquisite face soft with passion. But she still held back.

Dammit, he was the classic case of a man caught in his own trap. In teaching her to want him, he found himself wanting her. Quite desperately. No, by heaven, if anyone was going to break through Susannah's skittish reserve and enjoy all her sweet, untapped passion, it was damned well going to be him.

"Ahh. Well, in that case the field's wide open, isn't it?" Pierce challenged, smiling, his spirits once more restored.

Jake answered with a level look, and Pierce laughed.

The instant she opened the door to Jake that evening, Susannah sensed his strange mood. He was quiet, his face grim and remote, and underneath his forbidding expression she detected a seething restlessness.

"Is something wrong?" she questioned, looking at him askance when they were settled in the low-slung car.

"No. Nothing."

She sighed and fell silent. All the way to Jones Hall neither said a word. Susannah sat through the first half of the play without being aware of what was taking place on stage. She was so concerned about Jake's strange behavior she could concentrate on nothing else.

His dark mood had not lifted by intermission. If anything, it worsened when Pierce Sorrenson appeared out of the crowd.

"Well, well. We meet again." Pierce picked up Susannah's hand and brought it to his lips, his blue eyes twinkling at her over the top. "Twice in one day. It must be fate."

Susannah smiled and glanced at Jake. He watched Pierce through narrowed eyes. A tiny muscle along his jaw rippled.

"And may I say, you look magnificent." Ignoring Jake, he continued to hold Susannah's hand and smile at her with warm appreciation. "That shade of green goes perfectly with your eyes."

"Why... thank you." Susannah glowed. This was her first evening at Jones Hall, and she had bought a new dress specifically for the occasion, one she could ill afford. Marta, who had helped Susannah dress and subdued her riotous curls into an elegant chignon, had surveyed their handiwork with tears in her eyes, but Jake's only reaction had been a long, head-to-toe, brooding look.

"Where are your seats?" Pierce inquired. Then he went on before Susannah could answer, "Never mind. You must join my mother and me in our box. We have the best seats in the house."

Pierce reached for Susannah's elbow to escort her, but Jake stepped between them and slipped an arm around her waist. "Back off, Sorrenson. If I have to warn you again to stay away from Susannah I'll rearrange that aristocratic nose of yours."

"*Jake!*"

Pierce chuckled. "You'd do it, too, wouldn't you? You damned ruffian."

"You can bet on it."

"Jake, stop this!"

Jake looked down at Susannah's distressed face, and something dangerous leaped in his eyes. Without a word, he turned and headed for the exit, hauling her along with him.

"Jake! Stop! What are you doing? Where are you taking me?"

He didn't answer, and from the set of his jaw Susannah thought it wise not to press the matter. Already the people nearby had fallen quiet and were watching their departure with interest as Jake waded through the crowd like Moses parting the Red Sea. Holding her head high, Susannah stared straight ahead and tried to match her steps to his, which wasn't easy, since he was lifting her off the floor with each long stride.

He remained stony-faced and silent while they waited for the valet to bring the car around, and all during the drive back to her house. At first Susannah was confused and hurt, but as the silent miles mounted, those feelings turned to anger. When Jake braked to a stop in front of her house, she was out the door and through the front gate by the time he turned off the ignition.

"Susannah! Dammit, wait!"

"No."

From behind her came a blistering curse, followed immediately by heavy footsteps and the squeak of the gate. Susannah broke into a run, but he caught her halfway up the walk and swung her up in his arms.

"Put me down!" She twisted and kicked and pummeled his shoulders. "Did you hear me? I said put me down! I don't want to talk to you!"

"Good. Talking isn't what I had in mind."

"Jake Taggart, if you don't put me down this instant I'll scream for Marta."

"Marta's playing bingo at the Senior Citizens' Center. Remember? Now give me your key."

"No, I wo— Jake!" she wailed, when he dumped her on her feet and took her purse from her, fishing out the key himself.

When he had the door open, she shot him a disgruntled look and marched inside. He followed her in without a word. Coming to a halt in the middle of the living room, she whirled around, set to do battle, but his expression gave her pause. His gray eyes held a dangerous look, one every woman instinctively understood, regardless of experience.

Susannah felt a flutter in the region of her heart. She swallowed hard and tried to hold on to her anger. "I . . . I want you to go, Jake."

"Tough."

He stalked toward her, his gaze locked with hers.

Susannah backed up. "Stop it, Jake. You're scaring me."

He kept coming, his expression intent, and her heart seemed to leap right up into her throat.

She held her hands up to ward him off. "Jake, stop. You— Oh!" The backs of her legs hit the hassock, and as she began to topple, Jake grasped her shoulders.

He jerked her against his chest so hard, the pins anchoring her chignon went flying and her hair tumbled around her shoulders and down her back in a wild tangle of silver-gilt curls. Like a frightened filly, Susannah tossed back her head, her eyes wide, her neck a delicate arch of purest ivory, the pulse at its base fluttering wildly.

Jake went utterly still and stared down at her.

Susannah's heart pounded so hard her whole body shook with every heavy thud. She gazed up at Jake's dark face, excitement, fear and a terrible longing pouring through her. "Ja-Jake?" she whispered.

His nostrils flared and something flickered in his eyes as they focused on her parted lips. "Pierce Sorrenson is one of my best friends," he said in a gritty voice. "But when he touches you, I want to smash his face in."

Every bit of apprehension and lingering anger vanished, and Susannah's face softened. Was that it? That was the reason for his black mood? Jealousy? She gazed at him in amazement. Jake was so strong, so self-assured, so...so tough, she had never thought of him being insecure about anything. Least of all her. Emotion squeezed Susannah's heart. She gave him a melting look and touched his cheek with her fingertips. "Oh, Jake."

At the gentle caress he sucked in his breath, and his hands tightened around her arms. "I want you, Susannah," he growled, and lowered his head.

He rocked his mouth over hers and kissed her with a slow, hot hunger that made Susannah weak. She shuddered and leaned into him, her fingers curling into the ruffled front of his evening shirt as waves of pleasure rolled over her.

Jake's hands roamed over her back, pressing her closer, as though he would absorb her into his being. His lips rubbed and nibbled, his tongue stroked. For all the passionate gentleness of the kiss, Susannah could feel how much his restraint was costing him. It was revealed in the thunderous beat of his heart beneath her palm and the fine tremors that ran through his straining muscles. The last vestige of fear melted, and her heart swelled with the knowledge that he would never hurt her.

After a moment Jake raised his head, and Susannah groaned, but the contact was broken only long enough for him to slant his mouth at a new angle. His arms tightened around her and his kiss grew firmer, hotter. With deep, slow strokes of his tongue, he told her what he wanted.

Susannah gasped at the unmistakable symbolism. Her body grew heavy and liquid, and a deep, hollow ache was building within her, making her restless.

Jake tore his mouth from hers and buried his face against the side of her fragrant neck. "I want you," he repeated, his voice rough with the guttural tone of fierce desire. His teeth nipped her neck, then he soothed the tiny pain with his tongue.

Susannah closed her eyes and shivered in ecstasy, and arched her neck to give him better access to the vulnerable curve of her throat. She felt his hot breath lightly touch her damp skin, awakening sensitive nerve endings. His hand moved up her side and boldly cupped her breast. "Did you hear me, Susannah?" he demanded hoarsely in her ear. "I want you."

"Ye-yes . . . I know."

"Do you want me?"

She shivered and moaned. Jake bit her earlobe and delved into the delicate shell with the tip of his tongue. "Do you?"

"Yes," she whispered. "Yes." Then, almost whimpering as Jake's thumb grazed her nipple, "Oh, yes! Yes!"

With a hard, triumphant laugh, Jake swept her up in his arms. Susannah gasped and clutched at his shoulders, her head swimming and her heart pounding as he strode through the dimly lit house to her bedroom.

He laid her down on the old-fashioned quilt that served as her bedspread. Quickly, he shed his coat and shoes and joined her on the bed, stretching out beside her, his leg hooked over hers. Susannah turned into his embrace eagerly, her expression rapt. Jake slipped his hand inside the low neckline of her dress, and everything inside Susannah went hot and liquid as his fingers stroked her bare flesh. She moaned and clung to him, and Jake gave a low growl.

"You like that, sweetheart? Tell me what else you like. What gives you pleasure, sweet Susannah?" he coaxed, stringing kisses along her collarbone as he pushed the dress off one shoulder. "Tell me, darling."

"I . . . I don't know."

"Don't be shy with me, sweetheart." Jake pushed the dress a little lower and rubbed his open mouth across the upper curves of her breasts. "I want to make this good for you. Tell me what you want."

Susannah's head moved restlessly on the pillow. "But I...I can't. I don't...know."

Jake went utterly still. He raised his head and stared down at her, his dark brows knitted together. "Are you—" he shook his head as though unable to accept the thought that buzzed in his mind "—are you saying that you're a *virgin?*"

Chapter Seven

Still caught in the dizzying grip of passion, Susannah made a frustrated sound and reached for Jake, but he pulled her arms from around his neck and withdrew farther.

"Answer me, dammit."

Susannah blinked. She felt on fire, her body buffeted by new sensations and taut with a coiling tension that demanded release. She gazed at him through a blur of desire and labored to sort out his words. "Wh-what?"

"Are you a virgin?"

The fierceness of his expression finally registered. Susannah blinked again, confused. "Yes. Of course I am. Y-you knew that."

His nostrils flared, and she felt him stiffen. She hadn't thought it possible, but his expression grew even more strained. "No, I didn't know. Perhaps I should have, but I didn't."

Apprehension began to creep in around the edges of Susannah's rosy cloud, and she looked at him with hurt in her eyes. "You mean ... You thought that I ..."

"For God's sake, Susannah. You're twenty-seven years old. Of course I thought you'd made love with a man before!"

"I...I see." She swallowed hard against the hurtful knot in her throat and asked quietly, "Does it matter that much?"

Jake stared down at her, and after a moment his jaw hardened. "No. It doesn't change a thing," he said in a strangely determined voice.

A small, glad cry escaped Susannah as he bent and took her mouth again. This time there was nothing gentle about his kiss. It was hot and ravaging, almost punishing. His teeth raked across her lower lip, and when she gasped, he thrust his tongue into her mouth and took his fill with bruising force.

Elation poured through Susannah, and she whimpered, partly in surprised reaction to his roughness, and partly in encouragement. Frantic, her body on fire, she writhed in his arms, pressing closer to his heat. She snatched at the pearl studs that fastened his shirtfront, popping them free, and she slid her hands beneath the edges. Her fingers threaded through the mat of hair and found the warm skin below, and she made a purring sound.

Jake jerked up the hem of her dress and slid his hand up her leg. A tremble shuddered through Susannah, and unconsciously her fingers flexed in the silky pelt of hair, her nails digging into his chest. When his hand reached the apex of her thighs, she caught her breath and stilled, the tension in her coiling tight.

With a violent curse, Jake snatched his hand from beneath her skirt, and in one continuous motion he rolled away from her and sat up on the side of the bed.

Startled, bereft, confused, Susannah gazed at his bowed back. He sat with his hands braced on his spread knees, and as she watched, a hard shudder shook his big frame. Without thought, she reached out and laid her hand on his back.

"Don't!" he snapped, and recoiled from her touch as though he'd received an electric shock. He glanced at her hurt face and cursed again, raking a hand through his hair. His shirt gaped, exposing his brawny chest. "I can't do this," he muttered violently. "I thought I could but I can't."

He lunged off the bed, grabbed his coat and stuffed his feet into his shoes.

"Jake!" Susannah cried. "Jake, please don't go. I love you, Jake."

He flinched and turned around, his expression pained. "I'm sorry, Susannah. This was a mistake."

"Jake!" Susannah jackknifed into a sitting position and held her hand out to him in supplication, but he had already disappeared through the door. A moment later she heard the front door slam, the sound a death knell to her heart. A powerful engine roared to life, and she closed her eyes. With a cry, she twisted around and flung herself facedown on the bed.

"Why, Jake?" she wailed against her pillow in a voice that wobbled with tears. "Why? *Why?*"

She cried long and hard—until her pillow was wet, until her throat was raw and her eyes were puffy and burning, until there was not another tear left in her to shed. Still sniffling, she pulled herself out of bed and padded through the house to check the doors and turn out all the lights. Then she returned to the bedroom, stripped off her clothes and tossed them over a chair with no regard whatsoever for the expensive dress. Like a zombie, she donned her cotton nightgown, crawled back into her bed and lay awake in the darkness, her thoughts tormenting her.

She loved Jake and she wanted him. It seemed a cruel irony that just when she had surrendered the last of her reservation and was ready to give her heart over to him completely, he changed his mind; he no longer wanted her.

Jake didn't love her. She had wondered, had even begun to hope, but now she knew that he didn't. His reaction when she had blurted out her feelings for him told her so more plainly than words ever could. And surely a man who loved a woman would be happy to learn that she had never been with another man. Not furious.

She supposed he was behaving honorably. Jake was not a man to take advantage of an inexperienced woman. He would go on his way unscathed, sure that he had done the right thing and there was no harm done. He probably thought that she would get over him, given time.

Susannah rolled over onto her side and stared into the darkness. She sighed, her breath shuddering in sharp little gasps, the pathetic aftermath of tears. If only she could get over him.

Jake stomped on the brakes and brought the Porsche to a jarring stop at the traffic light. He drummed his fingers for three seconds then brought his fist down hard on the steering wheel. A virgin! Dammit to hell!

It shouldn't have made any difference. Marianne had been a virgin when Philip had seduced her. Actually, seducing Susannah and walking out once she was pregnant would have evened the score all the more and made his revenge just that much sweeter. An eye for an eye, so to speak.

Damn. Jake exhaled heavily and raked his hand through his hair. The problem was, he just couldn't do to Susannah what Philip had done to Marianne. Once he'd gotten to know her, he'd felt bad about hurting her at all, but at least he'd been able to tell himself that she was a woman, not an innocent girl.

The traffic light turned green and the driver behind Jake honked. "Keep your shirt on," Jake muttered, glaring at the impatient bozo in the mirror. He drove on, his mouth set in a grim line. Aw, hell, who was he kidding? He doubted that he could've carried through with the plan anyway. It wasn't Susannah's virginity that had stopped him. It was Susannah. He liked her, dammit!

Contrary to what he'd expected, she was sweet and sensitive and generous—a thoroughly nice person. Restful, too. Once he'd gotten her to loosen up she'd turned out to be a good conversationalist, but she wasn't a woman to chatter incessantly. He had enjoyed being with her. He hadn't expected to, but he had. He even looked forward to spending his evenings and weekends with her. There was a serenity and a softness about Susannah that he found soothing. God knew, she was too good a person to be stuck with relatives like Nathan and Philip.

Just thinking of the pair made Jake furious. He'd been so close to finally paying them back. So close.

Jake sighed and rubbed the back of his neck. He wondered how he could ever have thought he could go through with his scheme in the first place? Hell, he just didn't have it in him to do that to a woman—*any* woman, but especially not Susannah. And as long as he was being honest, he might as well admit that he could never abandon a child he had fathered, either.

As bad as he hated to, it looked as though he was going to have to give up on using Susannah to strike back at Nathan.

Unless...

No, he couldn't do that. Jake shifted uncomfortably and pushed the thought aside, but it kept coming back. Damn Pierce, anyway, Jake thought furiously, for putting the idea in his mind.

He drove on for several more blocks, his expression thoughtful. Still... there was something to be said for it.

First of all, he wouldn't have to cut Susannah out of his life, or set her adrift to cope with the likes of Pierce Sorrenson. And that devil would be after her like a shot; Jake knew Pierce.

Jake drummed his fingers on the steering wheel. It wouldn't all be one-sided, either. He would take care of her. Give her everything she deserved to have. A hard smile pulled at his mouth. And the best thing was, Nathan would be livid. Jake Taggart was the last man on earth he would want for a son-in-law.

Susannah was still awake, staring dry-eyed at the shadows on the ceiling, when a horrendous pounding on her front door startled her out of her painful thoughts.

What on earth? She sat up with a jerk, her heart beginning to pound. Was it Marta? Was something wrong?

Susannah scrambled out of bed and ran barefoot through the dark house, her long nightgown billowing out behind her like a ship's sail. At the door she reached for the knob, but at the last second she had the presence of mind to check the action. She leaned in close to the wooden panel and called cautiously, "Who's there?"

"Jake."

Susannah stiffened and stepped back. What was he doing back there? She had just gotten herself under control; she didn't want to go through all that again. Hadn't he hurt her enough?

"Susannah," he commanded in a low voice when she made no move to open the door. "Let me in. I have to talk to you."

Sighing, she rested her forehead against the door. If there was one thing she'd learned about Jake, it was that he never gave up. He would wait all night if he had to. Or break down the door. Resigned, she flipped on the light, unlocked the door and opened it, stepping aside to let him enter.

The instant Jake was inside, he turned and searched her face. "Are you all right?"

She glanced at him, then averted her eyes. "Yes. What do you want?" She kept her face cold and remote, her voice clipped.

"Susannah, I'm sorry—"

"Just say what you came to say, then please leave."

Several seconds of silence ticked by, and she could feel his gaze on her. "All right. I want you to marry me, Susannah."

That was the last thing she expected. Her head whipped around. "*Marry* you! But..." Vaguely, she gestured toward the bedroom, then shook her head as though to clear it. "But you..."

"Susannah, I overreacted, I'll admit. When I found out you were an innocent it threw me. But I've been thinking about that—and about us—and I think the best thing would be for us to get married."

Susannah stared at him. It was not exactly what you would call a romantic proposal. Still...she couldn't deny that a part of her wanted to throw herself in his arms and yell, "Yes! Yes! Yes!" She loved Jake and she wanted, more than anything, to spend the rest of her life with him. But another part of her hung back, afraid of being hurt more than she already had been.

"Why?" she managed to ask.

"It's either that or we call it quits. This thing between us is too strong for us to keep on the way we have been. Sooner or later we're going to end up in bed. I believe tonight proved that." He gave her a direct look, and Susannah cursed her fair complexion, feeling heat rise in her face. "Since you're not the kind of woman for an affair and I don't take advantage of innocents, I don't see any other choices for us."

"I see." What had she expected? A declaration of undying love? He had already shown her that he didn't return her feelings.

Susannah felt fragile and vulnerable. Instinctively, she crossed her arms over her midriff, but when Jake's gaze lowered to where the semitransparent material pulled taut across her breasts, she quickly unfolded her arms and turned away, walking to the center of the living room. "That doesn't seem like a very good reason to get married."

"There are others. We get along well. We like the same things. I think we could have a good life together." He walked over to her and hooked his forefinger beneath her chin, tipping her face up. "You said you love me, Susannah," he whispered. "Did you mean it?"

She winced at the humiliating reminder and closed her eyes. She was tempted to lie and tell him no, but she couldn't. Besides, what would be the point? She'd never been good at hiding her feelings. It amazed her that he hadn't realized the truth before now. "Yes. I meant it."

"Then marry me, sweetheart," he cajoled. "I'll be a good husband. You can trust me to be faithful. When I make a commitment I keep it. I'll take good care of you, Susannah, and I'll do my best to make you happy. I swear it."

He slipped his arms around her and pulled her close. As naturally as breathing, Susannah nestled against his chest and looped her arms around his middle, her soft curves adjusting to the hard contours of his muscular frame like the missing piece of a puzzle sliding into place.

Jake made a sound of pleasure and nuzzled his cheek against the top of her head, the hint of whisker stubble along his jaw snagging the silky strands. "You see how perfectly we fit. We were made for each other." He lowered his head, and she felt his breath in her ear as he whispered huskily, "We'll be good together, honey. Better than you could possibly imagine."

Susannah shivered at the hot, honeyed words, pleasure running through her. He wasn't being fair; how could she think clearly when her mind was filled with the shocking, enticing images he was deliberately evoking?

"I want you, Susannah," Jake murmured in a low seductive voice that made her body quicken. "I want to make love to you until you scream with pleasure. You want that, too, don't you, honey?"

Yes! Susannah cried silently. Yes! She did not have to experience sex with Jake to know that he would be a wonderful lover. She had known that from the first. He could make her body sing with just a touch. But there was more to marriage than lovemaking.

Jake didn't love her; conspicuously absent from his reasons for wanting to marry her had been any mention of his feelings for her. He would give her companionship and physical satisfaction and all the financial security anyone could hope for, but would that be enough?

There was always the possibility, of course, that he would come to love her, given time. But she would only have that time if she accepted his offer. If she refused him he would disappear from her life forever.

In marrying him she would be taking a tremendous risk. He might never love her and she could end up as unhappy and alone as her mother had. But then . . . if she didn't take the chance, she would definitely end up that way, because Susannah knew that she would never love anyone else, not as she loved Jake.

"Say yes, baby," Jake urged, and Susannah squeezed her eyes shut, melting inside.

Finally, gathering her courage, she stepped back out of his arms and looked at his dark, hard face. She took a deep breath. "All right. Yes. I'll marry you."

His only reaction was a brief flare of something in his eyes that vanished almost before it began. Then he pulled her back into his arms and kissed her, a long, drugging kiss full of sensual promise that made the world tilt and her head spin. When he released her and stepped back, Susannah clutched at him to steady herself.

Her dazed expression drew a crooked, purely masculine smile from Jake. He gave her another swift kiss, but when she swayed toward him, he turned her around and gave her a little shove toward the bedroom. "Go on now and get dressed so we can go."

"Go? Go where?"

"To get married."

Susannah's jaw dropped. "*Tonight?* Jake, we can't get married tonight! Just like that."

"Sure we can. There's a flight to Las Vegas in a little over an hour. If we hustle we can make it."

"But . . . but what about your sister? Don't you want her to be there when you get married? And then there's Marta, and Alice and—"

"A big fuss is precisely what I don't want," Jake interrupted. "I'm not waiting for Marianne and Grant to get back from Europe. That'll be weeks. Besides, I just sent my nephew over there to join them. For months he's been looking forward to seeing Europe. He'll be mad as a hornet if they cut the trip short.

"We've made the decision to get married—and I don't see any point in delaying," he said in that decisive tone that Susannah had come to know well. He fixed her with a piercing look. "I want you, Susannah. And I don't intend to wait another day."

Susannah shivered—all the way from her head to her bare feet. "I'll go get dressed," she whispered.

After that, everything happened so fast that Susannah was left reeling. The flight to Las Vegas, checking into the hotel, getting the license, the ceremony—it all seemed like a dream.

Except, of course...the ring on the third finger of her left hand was real. Very real.

Tentatively, Susannah touched the wide band, her shaking fingertip running over the glittering diamonds that encrusted it. In nine incredibly short hours—hours that had zipped by in a blur of colors and sounds and motion—she had totally and irrevocably changed her life. Now, here she was, in the middle of the day, in the opulent bathroom of a honeymoon suite...a brand-new, extremely nervous bride. Susannah glanced at the closed door and licked her lips. With an impatient groom waiting in the next room.

She checked her reflection in the wall of mirrors and winced. Dear heaven, she was all eyes and hair. Her face was a pale oval in a paler cloud of silvery curls. The only bit of color on her was her wide green eyes. Even her nightgown was white.

The modest garment was one she had brought with her, hastily stuffed into her bag, along with the few other items that Jake had given her time to pack. Susannah frowned and tried to pluck the cotton cloth away from her body. Funny, she'd never noticed before how thin it was. The long, sleeveless gown hung in voluminous folds from an embroidered yoke, the design the very essence of modesty, but the shadowy aureoles of her nipples were clearly visible through the delicate batiste, and every movement provided a glimpse of peach-tinted flesh.

With a groan, Susannah turned away from her reflection. She was being foolish. Only a few hours ago she had been melting in Jake's arms, eager for his lovemaking. She grasped the doorknob, took a deep breath, forcibly subduing her shakiness, and opened the door.

Jake felt as though he'd taken a blow to the chest from a sledgehammer when Susannah stepped through the door. He had never seen anything so beautiful in his life. She stood there ramrod straight, her moonbeam hair rioting around her shoulders and down her back. A shy smile wavered on her lips, but he could see the apprehension in her eyes, and he felt a sharp tug on his heartstrings.

The virginal gown covered her from collarbone to toes, but somehow it managed to be outrageously sexy. The delicate material fluttered around her like a tantalizing cloud, enticing and insubstantial, driving him crazy with thoughts of the warm, womanly body underneath.

He walked toward her, and he saw the fear in her eyes as her gaze flickered downward over the robe belted loosely around his waist and the wedge of bare chest exposed between the broad lapels. The hotel routinely furnished the thick terry-cloth garment, and he had worn it only as a concession to her inexperience. Now he was glad he had.

When he stopped in front of her, he saw her eyes widen and the almost imperceptible way she tensed. He smiled and cupped her face with his hand. "You don't have to be afraid, honey."

"I'm not," she lied with a shaky smile. "Just a little nervous, is all."

Jake looked at her tenderly. Her vulnerability and her brave front tugged at his heart. At the same time her beauty and sweet womanly scent were having a drastic effect on another part of his body.

She smelled of soap and bath talc and some sort of feminine shampoo. The moist air roiling from the bathroom carried the same enticing scents. "I won't hurt you, Susannah," he whispered, rubbing his thumb back and forth across her soft lower lip. "I don't ever want to hurt you. I want you to remember that. Always."

"I will," she promised, and with a gentle smile she placed her hand on top of his and turned her face into his palm, her green eyes glowing with trust and love as she pressed a lingering kiss there.

Jake caught his breath. The touch of her warm, incredibly soft lips against his skin seemed to set off an explosion in his heart. With a growl, he swooped her up in his arms and carried her to the bed, his gaze locked all the while on her lovely face. His bent knee sank into the mattress, and he lowered her onto it as though she were the most precious thing in the world.

Stretching out beside her, he took her into his arms. With a hand that was not quite steady, he stroked her glorious hair away from her temple and studied her face. In his lifetime he'd made love to many women, but he couldn't remember ever feeling this way before. His heart was pounding and his chest was so tight he could barely draw breath. He actually felt shaky. Yet at the same time he felt energized, wired, able to leap tall buildings in a single bound.

Jake smiled at the foolish thought. Yeah, sure, Taggart. Your insides are quivering so much at the moment you couldn't leap a bug on the sidewalk.

His smile faded and was replaced by a slight, puzzled frown, but he continued to stroke her hair, her cheek, the silky arch of her eyebrow. What was it about this particular woman that affected him so?

"Jake?" The tinge of worry in Susannah's voice snapped him out of his musings, and he lifted her hand to his lips and returned the salute she had given him, watching her lovely face soften and heat as he pressed his mouth to the center of her palm. His teeth raked the sensitive flesh and she said his name on a wisp of breath. With the tip of his tongue, he laved the same spot. Air hissed from between her slightly parted lips. A soft mist of passion clouded her green eyes and they grew heavy lidded. "Oh, Jake. Jake."

Lord, he loved watching her. She was so incredibly responsive; from just the touch of his mouth on her palm she was becoming aroused. And she was so open and honest with her emotions. Every reaction, every nuance of feeling

she experienced showed in her face, and she made no effort to hide any of it.

He nibbled each of her fingers, and she moaned softly.
Then slowly, deliberately, his eyes trained on her enrap-
tured face, he licked the delicate skin between the base of
each finger. The moan became a whimper and her lashes
drifted down as she moved restlessly and pressed closer to
him. "Jake, please!"

Whether Susannah's plea was a cry for mercy or more of
the sensual pleasure, Jake didn't know, but the soft words
snapped his control. With a low growl, he pulled her close,
looming half over her, taking her avid mouth with a hunger that demanded more and more.

They kissed endlessly, deeply, their bodies straining together. Jake stroked and fondled her, building her desire
with such consummate skill that she scarcely noticed when
he lifted the nightgown over her head and tossed it aside,
or when his robe followed.

All Susannah felt was pleasure, the sharp, sweet tugging
of his mouth on her nipple, the feel of his hands roaming
her stomach, her breasts, her legs, the tactile enjoyment to
be found in the exploration of a loved one's body, the bliss
of heated flesh melding and rubbing. Susannah writhed in
ecstasy, loving his unique scent, the slightly salty taste of his
skin, the feel of his hard, muscular body pressing against
her soft curves.

With care and patience, Jake aroused Susannah to such
a fever pitch of desire she experienced only the slightest
flutter of anxiety when he moved over her and nudged her
legs apart, and that was quickly banished under the drugging effect of his kiss. Her body was hot and liquid, eager,
and when he claimed her, she was so shattered by the beauty
of being one with the man she loved that the brief moment
of pain was quickly forgotten.

All Susannah felt was love, and a deep joy at the absolute rightness of it. And when the pleasure grew and grew

and the end came with its exquisite, almost unbearable ecstasy, her entire being, her world, her universe was reduced to that moment...and the man she held so tightly in her arms.

Chapter Eight

Susannah awoke to a spectacular sunset of crimson, gold and mauve. She blinked and gazed muzzily out the balcony doors at the colorful display, not knowing, for a moment, where she was. Her sleepy gaze fell on her nightgown and the terry-cloth robe lying in a crumpled heap in the middle of the floor. With a start, she remembered, and her eyes opened wide. She turned her head toward the other side of the bed, and her heart leaped.

Jake lay propped up on one elbow, watching her.

Waking up in bed with a man was a new experience for Susannah, and, though she loved Jake dearly, embarrassed heat swamped her body from head to toe. She felt as though she were glowing. "Hi," she murmured shyly.

Something flickered in his eyes at the husky sound, but his intent expression did not alter. "Hi." He brushed a pale curl off her cheek and trailed his forefinger down her arm. "How do you feel? Sore?"

The blush, which had begun to fade, heated up again. She tucked the sheet more securely under her armpits and stared at her hands clasped together across her stomach. "No. Well...a little." She plucked at the sheet. "But if you want to... That is...I wouldn't mind..."

At Jake's soft chuckle her skin sizzled. Even her earlobes felt on fire.

He leaned over and kissed her lingeringly, and Susannah sighed and cupped the back of his head, her fingers sinking into his hair. "I want," he whispered against her lips. "Very much. But I know you're still tender. I can wait."

He gave her another quick kiss and rolled from the bed before Susannah could wrap her arms around his neck. He stretched, and she watched in fascination the ripple and bunch of muscles across his back and bare buttocks. "Anyway, we don't have time if we're going to catch Cosby's eight o'clock show."

Clutching the sheet to her, Susannah sat up, her eyes round. "You got tickets? But how? Don't his performances sell out weeks in advance?"

"Money." Jake turned and gave her a chilling look. "You'd be surprised how many strings it can pull. I learned a long time ago, the hard way, that money means power. Without it, you're a helpless victim."

Magnificently naked, he strode into the bathroom and slammed the door, leaving Susannah staring after him, bewildered and uneasy. What on earth had she done to set off that cold fury? One minute he had been tender and considerate, the next icy, his hard face dark and remote. She didn't understand.

To her relief, when Jake emerged twenty minutes later, the strange mood had passed.

Susannah thoroughly enjoyed the show, though she was a bit shocked by the scantiness of the costumes worn by the dancers and showgirls. Afterward, she and Jake spent a few hours in the casino, where he attempted, in vain, to teach her the finer points of roulette and black jack. Susannah was bemused by it all—the "clunk-clunk-clunk" of coins pouring from the slot machines, the whir of roulette wheels, the flutter of cards and the click of chips, the often raucous shouts of the crowds around the crap tables. It was a new, alien world to Susannah, and she took it all in with wide-eyed wonder.

With typical beginner's luck, Susannah finished the evening a winner. Jake looked on indulgently while she cashed in her chips, chuckling at her astonishment over the amount she had won.

"This can't be right," she said, turning to him in slack-jawed shock, clutching the stack of hundred dollar bills. "I didn't have that many chips."

"Yes, but they were mostly greens." When her expression remained blank, he sighed and explained patiently, "Susannah, the green chips are worth a hundred dollars each."

Grinning, Jake hooked his forefinger under her sagging jaw and lifted it. "Come on now, close your mouth and put your winnings in your purse. That's a good girl."

"A hundred dollars," she finally managed to croak, docilely allowing him to steer her out of the casino. Susannah moaned and placed her hand over her eyes. "I was betting hundreds of dollars at a time. You *let* me bet hundreds of dollars at a time!" she accused, shooting him an annoyed look, her voice gaining strength as shock turned into ire.

"Sure, why not? Anyway, I assumed you knew how much you were betting."

"I thought all chips were worth a dollar," she groaned.

"Didn't you wonder why they were different colors?"

"Not really. I just thought they were pretty."

Jake shook his head and bundled her into the elevator.

On the way up, her distress vanished like a puff of smoke when it finally hit her that she had just won several thousand dollars. Jake leaned against the elevator wall with his arms crossed over his chest, grinning, and watched her excitement grow. When they got off on their floor, Susannah practically danced a jig down the hall.

In the suite, she ran into the bedroom and dumped the money out of her purse onto the bed. "Will you just look at that! I can't believe it!"

"Susannah, did you understand any of the games you played?"

"No, but what does it matter? I won! Do you realize this money will take a sizable bite out of Mother's medical bills?"

Jake's pleasure over her childlike joy vanished. He crossed the room in three long strides and spun her around to face him. His hard face looked like a thundercloud.

"You will not spend one penny of that money on those bills," he decreed, enunciating each word slowly and distinctly through clenched teeth. "Do you understand? Not one penny."

"But, Ja—"

"*I'll* take care of your mother's medical expenses. As soon as we get home I want you to give me all the statements. First thing Monday morning, I'll see that they're paid in full."

"I can't let you do that!" Susannah cried, appalled and touched by his generosity.

"The hell you can't. You're my wife now. I'm going to take care of you from now on. That means paying your debts, as well as a lot of other things."

"No. That's impossible. I'll—"

"Susannah, the matter is settled."

She opened her mouth, but shut it again when his eyes narrowed. Stymied, she searched his face and sighed. He had that determined look again, and she knew she could argue until the sky turned green, but he would not give up. "Oh, Jake." She placed her hands on either side of his face and gazed into his eyes earnestly. "I didn't marry you for your money."

He saw the love in her eyes, her concern, and felt something crack and shift inside him. His hands loosened, and he gently massaged away his cruel grip. "I know," he said in a softer voice. Three months before he would not have believed her, but he did now. For that matter, there was no woman of his acquaintance that he would have believed that of—except Susannah.

The irony of it left a bitter taste in his mouth.

"I never thought you were mercenary. I know you're proud and independent. And I know how hard you've had to work these past ten years, but those days are over. The fact is, you *have* married a man with money, and I damn well intend to use some of it to pay those bills you've been struggling with for so long."

"Oh, Jake." This time her voice held aching tenderness, and her eyes filled with tears. Her chin wobbled, and she pressed her lips together to stop their shaking. The melting look in her eyes made his heart squeeze. "You're so wonderful."

Jake's fingers tightened around her arms again, and his jaw clenched. Guilt twisted his gut, but he fought against it. He couldn't—he *wouldn't*—go soft now.

"Don't put me on a pedestal, Susannah," he warned in a grim voice. "I'm not wonderful or kind or any of those things. I'm just a man exercising my husbandly rights." His gaze dropped from her misty eyes to her lips, soft and slightly parted and still quivering sweetly. His eyelids grew heavy, and his head began a slow descent. "All of them," he murmured against her mouth.

He felt the tremor that ran through her, heard the little hitch in her breath, and desire streaked through him.

Susannah sighed, and he caught the sound with his mouth. He slipped his arms around her, molding her to him, widening his stance to bring her closer still. His open mouth rocked and rubbed over hers, a wet, hot torment that devoured and tantalized at the same time. Susannah whimpered and sagged against him, twining her arms around his neck, her body going boneless, flowing against his.

The eager openness of her response fired his passion. He eased down the zipper at the back of her dress and tumbled with her to the bed. "I'll be easy with you, sweetheart," he promised huskily against her neck, while his big hands worked the dress off her shoulders and down her arms. "I promise. But I have to love you again."

"Jake." His name came out on a sigh, a zephyr of sound rich with emotion.

Jake shoved the dress down, and Susannah lifted her hips to allow him to remove it. He sent the silky garment sailing. Moments later her slip followed and drifted to the carpet with a silent flutter. Jake reached to unclip her bra, but his hand stilled in midair.

He stared. She lay there, clad in only her panties and bra, two miniscule scraps of black silk and lace against her smooth ivory skin, her glorious hair spread around her head and shoulders in a silvery cloud. His breath caught, and his blood pounded through his body like a runaway locomotive. Never had he seen anything so beautiful . . . or so desirable. And she was his.

The full reality of that hit him only then, and with a stunning force that would have staggered him had he been on his feet. Until Susannah, Jake had never made love to a virgin; he'd never wanted to. When a man initiated a woman in the act of love, Jake felt he owed her more than just a roll in the hay, and he had never wanted that kind of responsibility or commitment. So he had taken his pleasure with experienced women.

Suddenly, however, he was fiercely glad that Susannah had never belonged to another man. He knew, without a single doubt, that she was his, and only his, and the knowledge made him feel fiercely possessive.

"Susannah," he whispered almost reverently, scarcely aware of speaking. Turning the hand that hovered over the front closure of her bra, he stroked the backs of his knuckles in a feather-light touch along the upper curves of her breasts swelling over the top of the lacy garment. The contrast of his dark-skinned hand against her pearly flesh was faintly shocking, and extremely arousing, and Jake's nostrils flared.

Susannah closed her eyes and shivered, and a raw pleasure like nothing Jake had ever known ripped through him. On fire and shaking with savage desire, he watched her lashes flutter open.

She smiled and reached for him, her eyes heavy-lidded and luminous with love and passion. "Jake. Oh, Jake, darling."

The quiet aftermath had a dreamy contentment to it that was new to Jake. Staring at the shadows across the dimly lit room, he absently rubbed his hand up and down Susannah's arm. She lay with her head on his shoulder, her hand resting on his chest, one finger lazily trailing through the mat of dark hair. The clean, floral scent of her shampoo drifted to him.

He could feel her moist breath fluttering across his skin, the feathery tickle of her hair, her soft breasts pressed against his side. From outside came the faint "whoop-whoop-whoop" of a siren in the distance. The air conditioning clicked on with a soft whir. Already it had dried the sweat from their bodies, except along his side where their naked skin melded together.

Something crackled under Jake's leg. He glanced down at the foot of the bed, and grinned. Wrinkled one-hundred-dollar bills lay scattered all over the bed. They had been so wrapped up in each other they had forgotten all about her winnings.

"Susannah?"

"Hmm?"

"I meant it about paying off your debts."

The finger twining in his chest hair stilled. She sighed. "I know. I'm sorry if I sounded ungrateful. It's just that for so long I've been solely responsible for myself and Mother, and the cost of caring for her, that it's difficult to turn loose."

"I know." His hand moved back and forth along her arm. "You must have had to quit college early to take care of her."

"Hmm. I had to drop out before my second year was over."

"Couldn't your father have helped you?" he asked, forcing a casual tone. He waited for her answer, every muscle in his body taut. During the past weeks, while he had wooed her, he had carefully avoided any mention of her father or brother, or even Zach's Corners. He hadn't wanted to risk tipping his hand before he was ready.

He felt rather than heard her chuckle. "I'm afraid my parents' divorce was a bitter one—at least on my father's side. He never forgave Mother for walking out. Or me for going with her," she added quietly.

"He didn't finance college?"

She shook her head. "He would have if I had moved home, but I couldn't leave my mother."

Jake let a minute tick by in silence while he continued his hypnotic stroking. "When we get back, we'll have to let him know about our marriage, you know. How do you think he'll take the news?"

"I don't imagine he'll care one way or another," she said over a yawn. "We've grown apart. We hardly ever see each other."

Jake frowned. When she'd said she wasn't close to her father, he hadn't thought much about it. He assumed she meant their personalities clashed, but this sounded more serious than that.

He felt the flutter of her eyelashes against his shoulder and glanced down. Eyes closed, she drifted into sleep while he watched. A warm feeling enveloped him, and he smiled. With her hair tumbled and wild and her mouth slightly parted, she looked about sixteen.

No, she had to be wrong. Perhaps she'd quarreled with Nathan over something and they hadn't made up yet. She probably had her feelings hurt, but he couldn't believe her relationship with her father was as remote as she made it sound. Not even a sorry bastard like Nathan Dushay would turn his back on a daughter as sweet as Susannah.

The news of their marriage was met with varied reactions.

At first, Marta was angry and a little hurt because they had eloped. Susannah had insisted on leaving her a note before they left Houston, so that she wouldn't worry. When she'd called home after the ceremony, her old friend had still been in a bit of a snit over the whole thing, but by the time Susannah and Jake returned on Sunday night at the end of their brief two-day honeymoon, Marta had calmed down.

Of course, she claimed that she was not in the least surprised. "Didn't I say that you'd meet a Scorpio who would play an important part in your life?" she asked with a smug grin. "The minute I laid eyes on Jake Taggart I knew he was the one. I keep telling you, child, the stars don't lie. Maybe you'll pay attention to me from now on," she added, giving an offended sniff and folding her arms beneath her ponderous bosom.

The news sent a shock wave through the ranks of Jetco employees, especially among the women. Comments ran the gamut from a wailed "Susannah, how could you steal that gorgeous man right from under our noses!" to a dreamily sighed "Oh, you lucky thing, you," to a delightedly whooped "Hot damn!"

The men, after their initial astonishment, offered hearty congratulations to Jake and complimented him on his choice of bride. Her, they treated with new deference and respect, even a touch of wariness. Evidently they thought, to Susannah's amusement, that in her new position as Jake's wife she carried a lot more clout than she'd had as executive assistant, and all were anxious to be on her good side.

Alice's first comment was an unruffled, "Well, it's about time. I knew the minute I met her that Susannah was perfect for you." That was quickly followed up by a sour look and a disgustedly muttered, "I suppose this means I'll have to find myself another assistant."

Before Susannah could assure her otherwise, Jake answered, "Yes. Susannah is going to be busy running our home. Besides, she may decide that she wants to go back to college," he added matter-of-factly, stunning his new bride.

In Las Vegas, during one of those quiet times when passions were slaked and they had lain in each other's arms, talking, Susannah had confessed her secret desire to become a writer and her deep disappointment over not being able to finish college.

She could barely recall the talk or exactly what she'd said, but evidently Jake remembered. Speechless, she gazed at him with tears in her eyes, her heart so full it felt as though it would burst. "Oh, Jake, I...I don't know what to say."

Her gratitude seemed to make him uncomfortable, especially with Alice watching them with that amused smirk. "There's no need to say anything. It's not that big a thing." He picked up the stack of mail from Alice's desk and walked into his office.

Susannah followed on his heels. "Jake, you can't just make a statement like that and expect me not to say anything. You have to at least let me thank you."

"No, I don't." When she opened her mouth to argue, he hooked his hand around the back of her neck and hauled her to him, cutting off her words with a kiss—a hard, devouring kiss that made her heart pound. When it ended, he lifted his head only partway and looked deep into her eyes. "I don't want you to thank me for every little thing I do for you, Susannah. Okay?"

"*Little* thing! Jake, nothing you've done for me so far has been a *little* thing. For heaven's sake! You've offered to pay off my mother's medical bills, you insist that I quit working and now you casually toss in college, too! So far, this has been a one-sided relationship, with you doing all the giving. It's not right."

"All right, look, you want to do something for me?" Jake pointed to the telephone on his desk. "Call your father and tell him you want to see him."

"Oh, good grief," Susannah said, thoroughly exasperated. "That's not doing something for you."

It took excruciating control for Jake to keep his face expressionless. *Oh, yes it is. Baby, you just don't know. Of course, if you did you wouldn't be here with me now. You would have run, as far and as fast as you could, a long time ago.*

"Yes it is. I won't feel right about this until I've told your father, face-to-face, that I've married his daughter." With a faint smile, Jake slid the telephone across the desk to her. "Make the call, Susannah."

"Oh, all right." Susannah sighed and picked up the receiver. "If it's that important to you."

"Don't tell him why you want to see him, just set it up."

Nodding, Susannah punched out the numbers, and Jake turned away and walked to the glass outer wall.

He stood absolutely still and stared out at nothing, his hands shoved into his pockets, his suit jacket open, the picture of casual unconcern. Every nerve in his body hummed. He waited, taut and eager, his gut twisting. It was going to happen.

"Hello. Mary?" he heard Susannah say behind him. "This is Susannah, I... Yes, I'm fine." A pause, and then, "I know, yes, it has been a long time. Uh, Mary, may I speak to my father, please?"

Jake closed his eyes, and his hands balled into fists in his pockets. At last, it was really going to happen! He drew in a deep breath, a vain attempt to ease the tightness in his chest. For years he'd dreamed of revenge, planned for it, worked to achieve the power to carry it through. And now, at long last, the wheels were in motion. The payback was almost here.

Jake glanced over his shoulder at Susannah. She had turned away from him and was talking softly into the telephone. His gaze went over her slender back and delicate shoulders, the tight little rear propped against the edge of the desk. In all of this, she was his only regret. Lord, he dreaded hurting her.

In the beginning he hadn't cared. The admission made him wince, but he faced the ugly truth of it. At first he'd even despised her—or rather, what she was: Nathan Dushay's spoiled, rich bitch of a daughter. Only she wasn't spoiled or rich or in any way bitchy. Susannah was sweet and sensitive and giving. And she was as much Nathan's victim as he and all the other Taggarts. She was a Taggart herself now.

Jake glanced at her again, and quickly returned his gaze to the traffic below. Damn, what a mess. In getting to know her, he'd found he liked her. And now, dammit, he... he *cared* for her. He wanted to protect her, make her life easier, give her everything she should have had all along. What he *didn't* want was to hurt her.

Fat chance, Taggart. Hurting Susannah was inevitable. Unavoidable. Even if he changed his mind about getting even—which he couldn't—it was too late.

The telephone receiver clattered against the base. Jake turned to find Susannah looking at him regretfully. "Well?"

"I'm sorry, Jake. Father isn't there. He left yesterday on a hunting trip somewhere in the Canadian Rockies." Susannah gestured toward the telephone. "That was his housekeeper."

"When will he be back?"

"Mary said they don't expect him for two weeks."

Disappointment settled over Jake, relaxing taut muscles and the coil of tension, but at the same time he was aware of a relief so great it almost buckled his knees.

"My brother, Philip, is running things while he's gone. He and his wife, Elaine, live in the house with my father. I didn't know whether you wanted to break the news to him or not, so I didn't set anything up. I can call back, if you'd like."

Jake waved the suggestion aside. "That's okay. We'll wait for your father to get back." He wanted them both there—Nathan *and* Philip—when he told them. He wanted to see the look on their faces. For that he could wait.

And in the meantime . . . he had Susannah.

Obeying an urge he didn't understand or question, Jake walked back to where Susannah stood and framed her face between his hands. He drank in the loveliness of her delicately sculpted features, her soft green eyes and flawless skin, and felt a strange warmth pouring through him. "Susannah," he whispered, and bent his head.

He kissed her with tender, smoldering passion and a depth of emotion that was painful in its sweetness. His heart contracted and his hands trembled against her cheeks. Against his palms he felt the same tiny vibrations rippling through Susannah. She swayed beneath the gentle assault and clutched at his waist for balance, her small hands sliding under his jacket and clenching his hard flesh, their warmth branding him through his cotton shirt.

He was touching her with only his hands and his lips, but Jake's body felt on fire. He wanted to lay her down, there on the floor of his office, and make slow, sweet love to her until neither of them could move, but he knew it was impossible.

Their lips clung as he ended the kiss and raised his head partway. Still framing her face with his hands, he stared at the delicacy of her closed eyelids, the crescents of feathery lashes on her cheeks, and her parted lips, still wet and shiny from his kiss.

Slowly, as though they were weighted with lead, her lashes lifted. Her eyes were bottomless pools of purest green. "What was that for?" she asked in a husky voice.

Jake wrapped his arms around her and pulled her close, cradling her against his chest. Rubbing his cheek against the top of her head, he rocked her from side to side. "No reason."

Against her silky hair he smiled ruefully. Except that he couldn't resist. And that he felt like he'd just received a reprieve. Because now he had two more weeks with her, two weeks to bind Susannah to him so tightly she would never be able to let go. No matter what.

That afternoon, Jake and Susannah left the office early and on the way home stopped by Jake's bank, where he opened a checking account for her with a starting balance that left her speechless.

Within the week she had a credit card for every major store in town as well as three national cards. As before, Susannah tried her best to express her feelings, but Jake flatly refused to listen to any of her attempts at thanks.

It was a pattern that repeated itself over and over in the weeks that followed. Jake spoiled her outrageously. He showered her with gifts, he was solicitous of her comfort and well-being and seemed concerned about her happiness, but whenever she tried to thank him, he cut her off brusquely and changed the subject.

Susannah wanted to believe that Jake would someday love her as she loved him, but even if that never happened, his actions told her that he did care about her. Surely a man wasn't so extravagantly generous with a woman unless he felt *something* for her.

Determined to make their marriage work, Susannah set about learning to be a full-time homemaker with the same gentle determination that she approached everything.

His luxury penthouse became her domain, and she took over the supervision of the housekeeper who came in three days a week, relieving the woman of most of the lighter tasks. Susannah happily did the grocery shopping and cooking, and all the mundane things that daily living required. It made her feel more like a wife to pick up Jake's dry cleaning and purchase his shaving cream. When Jake was in town, he came home each evening to a savory meal and a household that ran with well-oiled perfection.

Jake was a sensual man with a healthy sex drive. Hardly a night went by that he didn't make love to her. Susannah needed no previous experience to know that her husband was a superb lover. The physical side of their marriage was wonderful. But for all that, for all Jake's generosity and care, she sensed that something was not quite right.

She couldn't put her finger on it. On the surface their marriage was good, idyllic almost. Times of passion were balanced by times of contentment. There were lazy Sunday mornings when they ate breakfast late and read the paper together, often squabbling good-naturedly over the crossword puzzle, and quiet evenings at home spent just reading or watching television. Jake seemed to enjoy being with her; when he brought work home, he liked for her to keep him company, and she would curl up on the small sofa in the study with a book or her needlepoint.

Jake frequently told her, sometimes with words but more often with a sizzling look or a kiss, that he thought she was beautiful. When they were in bed together he whispered exciting, shocking things to her: how much he wanted her, all the things he wanted to do to her, how she made him feel. He told her how pretty he thought her slender body was, how much he loved her hair, how he loved burying his face in it and feeling the silky strands trail across his body. He told her how hungry he was for her, how at times at the office he couldn't work for thinking of making love to her. He did not, however, tell her that he loved her.

Love her or not, Jake was possessive of Susannah, flatteringly so. That, he had amply demonstrated the day Pierce Sorrenson learned of their marriage. The day after their return, Susannah had dropped by the office to clean out her desk, arriving only moments before the handsome banker. Alice had delighted in breaking the news to him.

"Married! My dear, I am heartbroken. Crushed, totally," he'd said in a mournful voice, made more pronounced by his soft Virginia drawl. "Since the day we met I have dreamed of sweeping you off your feet and taking you home to Mimosa as my bride. Mind you, the plantation isn't what it used to be, but you'd love the old place. It's the perfect setting for your beauty. Only Mama and Aunt Lilah live there now, and I'm quite sure that they would both adore you, as I do."

Pierce sighed with such exaggerated distress that Susannah almost laughed. Taking her hand, he held it against his cheek and gave her a sorrowful look that was totally spoiled by the devilish glint in his vivid eyes. "I had planned on continuing the Sorrenson dynasty with you. Can you imagine the children we could have produced together?"

Susannah laughed, blushing, but the sound died when Jake's voice intruded.

"What I can imagine, Sorrenson, is wringing your neck for having those kinds of thoughts about my wife."

Jake stood in the doorway of his office, his shoulder propped against the frame, watching Pierce with narrowed eyes, his face set in the hard mask that had caused more than one man to take to his heels. Pierce shot him an annoyed look.

"She wasn't your wife at the time, you pineywoods ruffian. And my intentions toward Susannah were strictly honorable."

Jake snorted. "Who are you kidding? You haven't had an honorable intention toward a woman since you were fourteen."

Ignoring the comment, Pierce stroked his forefinger down Susannah's satiny cheek and sighed again. "Such a pity."

Jake pushed away from the door and crossed the office. With no pretense at subtlety, he pulled Susannah out of Pierce's reach and tucked her against his side, his arm around her waist anchoring her there. "No touching. And that's your last warning."

Pierce grinned, a look of pure devilish glee lighting his face. "But surely I get to kiss the bride? It is tradition, you know."

Jake appeared to consider the request, then shrugged. "Sure," he replied smoothly. "If you don't mind risking life and limb, go right ahead."

"Jake!" Susannah gasped.

Pierce threw back his head and laughed. "All right. You don't deserve her, but I'll concede." Then he smiled tenderly at Susannah. "Just remember, my sweet, if this lout gives you a hard time or things don't work out, I'll be waiting."

"You're pushing it, Sorrenson," Jake warned in a deadly serious voice. "Friendship stretches just so far."

In the beginning Jake's possessiveness had given Susannah hope, but as the weeks passed, she began to wonder if the trait was simply a basic part of his makeup.

When she broached the subject with Marta, her answer was less than encouraging.

"It's possible," her friend reluctantly confirmed. "A Scorpio male is fiercely jealous of anything he believes to be his. But remember, Susannah, intensity is a major part of Jake's character. It also makes him capable of loving deeply."

It was a fragile hope on which to pin her future, but it was all Susannah had.

One of the little things that niggled at Susannah was Jake's refusal to notify his sister of their marriage.

"It'll keep," he said whenever she broached the subject. "Knowing Marianne, the minute she finds out, she'll hot-foot it back here to meet you. I don't want to interrupt their trip. This is supposed to be sort of a second honeymoon for her and Grant. I'll call them a day or so before they're due to return."

Susannah wasn't comfortable with the delay, but she supposed it made sense. Besides, she couldn't very well complain, since her own family had yet to be notified.

She had expected Jake to insist on meeting her father at the first opportunity. Nathan had been due back from his hunting trip three weeks ago, but so far Jake had made no effort to contact him. Whenever Susannah mentioned it, he always had an excuse why he could not make the trip to Zach's Corners just yet. She had begun to wonder if Jake was worried about meeting her family.

Heaven knew, Susannah was concerned over what Marianne's reaction would be. She knew that Jake and his sister were close and she could not help but wonder what the effect on her marriage would be if Marianne did not like her.

Luckily, most of the time Susannah was too busy to fret over the matter. She barely had a spare moment all summer.

With Marta's help, Susannah sifted through the accumulation of seventeen years in her old home. The task took weeks, mainly because everything she and Marta unearthed brought back a memory that had to be recalled and savored. Susannah finally ended up keeping only the best of her clothes and the keepsakes. All the furniture and the rest of the household items and clothes, including her mother's, went to a charity that came and hauled the stuff off.

When everything was gone, Susannah took one final tearful stroll through the empty duplex, running her hand over the faded wallpaper, gazing at the worn floors, touching the little marks on the inside of her closet door where her mother had charted her growth over the years. For Susannah, turning the key in the lock for the last time and handing it over to Marta marked, more than anything else had, the end of her old life and the beginning of her new one.

With that chore out of the way Susannah immediately began the process of enrolling in college.

In early August she sat cross-legged in the middle of the plush living room carpet, dressed in her oldest jeans and one of Jake's shirts, surrounded by brochures and class schedules, trying to figure out a way to fit another course into her already heavy classload. When the doorbell rang, she made an aggravated sound. Mrs. Murphy, the housekeeper was not there, and Jake was late getting home. She had no choice but to answer it.

Grumbling, Susannah jabbed her pencil into the cluster of curls piled carelessly on top of her head, hauled herself to her feet and padded, barefoot, to the door.

The doorbell rang again as she stepped into the entry-way. "Oh, hold your horses," Susannah muttered, and jerked the door open with more force than usual.

"Well, it's about ti—" The woman standing on the other side of the threshold stopped speaking abruptly and stared at Susannah with her mouth open.

The woman was gorgeous. With her dark hair, creamy skin and exotic pale eyes she looked like a sexy madonna. Susannah's first thought was she was probably one of Jake's old loves, and the rush of jealousy that followed set her teeth on edge.

"Who are you?" the woman demanded.

Susannah was about to ask the same of her when she noticed the man standing just behind the woman, staring at her as though he couldn't believe his eyes.

"Mr. Calloway!" Susannah exclaimed. At once, her stunned gaze jumped back to the woman, and her hand flew to her mouth. "Oh, my goodness," she managed weakly. "You must be Marianne."

Chapter Nine

"Susannah, what the devil are you doing here?" Grant Calloway demanded.

"You know this woman?" Marianne glanced over her shoulder at her husband, but her gaze quickly returned to Susannah, flickering over her with undisguised curiosity.

"Yes, she..." Darting a worried look at Marianne, Grant cleared his throat. "She, uh...she works at the office."

"Oh really? That's funny. I don't recall seeing you there. Although...there is something very familiar about you."

"I...I was hired just a day or so before you left for Europe." Susannah opened the door wider and stepped aside. "I'm sorry. I'm forgetting my manners. Won't you come in? Jake should be home any minute."

Marianne's delicate eyebrows rose at Susannah's casual use of Jake's name and her relaxed "at home" manner, but she accepted the invitation. Grant followed right on his wife's heels, shooting Susannah a strange, almost desperate look as he stepped past her.

Horribly conscious of her bare feet and sloppy garb, and the eyes boring into her back, Susannah led the way into the living room. "Won't you have a seat?" she invited, and began scooping up the brochures and papers from the floor. She turned, clutching the papers in one arm, and pushed a straggling curl off her cheek with her other hand. "I apologize for my appearance. I, uh…I've been busy and…well, I wasn't expecting company."

"Company? My, you have made yourself at home, haven't you?" Marianne's gaze flickered over her, and the corners of her mouth twitched. "I always did like that shirt on Jake."

Susannah felt a blush climb her neck. She groped for the words to explain, but before she could Grant jumped in.

"Never mind that. I want to know what you're doing here."

"Oh, darling, don't be obtuse. Isn't it obvious? She's living here. Although, I must say, this is not at all like Jake. He's had affairs before, of course, but he's never wanted a woman to move in with him."

Susannah gasped, her blush deepening, and Grant looked as though he had just received a fist to the stomach.

"Oh, my Lord. You're Jake's *mistress?*"

"No, I most certainly am not!" Susannah fired back before she thought. "I'm his wife!"

You could have heard a pin drop in the silence that followed. It lasted only a few seconds.

"Wife?" Marianne said weakly, and sat down hard on the sofa.

"No. No, that can't be," Grant insisted, but his tone lacked conviction. "Jake wouldn't—"

"Yes, I would."

At the sound of Jake's voice the three turned in time to see him stroll into the living room.

"Jake!" Marianne jumped up and threw herself into her brother's arms.

"Hi, sis. How was the trip?"

Jake paused just long enough to give her a hug and shake Grant's hand before going to Susannah. He put his arm around her shoulders and pulled her against his side. "You okay?" he asked gently. At her nod, he bent and kissed her full on the lips. He took his time about it, and when the kiss ended he turned back to the Calloways with a challenging look.

"Then it's true?" his sister asked in a small, shocked voice.

"It's true. Susannah and I were married five weeks ago."

The reactions of Jake's sister and brother-in-law did nothing to ease Susannah's mind.

"Oh, Jake," Marianne wailed. "How could you *do* this?"

Grant sank down in a chair and closed his eyes, looking like a man who had just received the shock of his life. Susannah could have sworn he even turned pale.

Jake skewered Marianne with a direct look. "Let me remind you, little sister, that I make my own decisions. I don't need your permission to do anything."

"But you knew that I would want to be there when you got married. I didn't even get to meet Susan beforehand."

"Susannah," Jake corrected. "And I don't need your stamp of approval on my choice of wife, either."

"But—"

"Look, Marianne, I didn't want a fuss. All right? Susannah and I decided to get married, so we did. End of discussion. Now we would like your good wishes, but if you can't give them—"

"Oh, Susannah! I'm so sorry!" Marianne exclaimed, rushing to embrace her. "You must think I'm terrible. Of course I'm happy for you both."

An uncertain smile wavered around Susannah's mouth, but Marianne caught her in an exuberant hug. "Welcome to the family." She gave her an enthusiastic squeeze and patted her back, while Jake and Grant talked together in hushed voices.

Grant's well wishes were much more constrained, but Susannah assumed that, like most men, he wasn't comfortable with expressing sentiment.

She was so relieved that the awkward encounter was over, she immediately invited Marianne and Grant for dinner. "It's nothing fancy—just pot roast and potatoes—but there's plenty and we'd love to have you join us."

"I don't think—"

"We'd love to, Susannah," Marianne accepted with alacrity, shooting her husband a speaking look.

Excusing herself, Susannah slipped away to change into a dress and run a brush through her unruly curls. She returned in less than ten minutes, feeling marginally more confident.

The meal was ready. Except for adding two place settings to the table, there was nothing left to do but serve it.

Throughout dinner Grant said little, but Marianne more than made up for her husband's reticence. She chattered away about their trip and about their sixteen-year-old son, Seth.

"On the way home we dropped him off at his grandparents' so he can spend these last couple of weeks before school starts with them. He's crazy about Grant's folks. *And* about their ranch." Marianne shot her husband a sparkling look and confided, "The Calloway men think they're putting one over on me, but I know that Seth's grandfather lets him drive the pickup over the ranch, even though he doesn't have his license yet."

In between anecdotes about her son and their trip, Marianne gently probed for information about Susannah and how she and Jake had become involved. Susannah didn't mind, and answered all her questions freely.

Except in looks and coloring, Marianne was the opposite of Jake, open and warm and softly feminine. By the end of the meal Susannah had high hopes of making a friend of her sister-in-law.

"I baked a rhubarb pie this afternoon. Would anyone care for some?" she asked when the men had finished eating.

"Rhubarb pie? Mmm, I love rhubarb pie," Marianne said.

"Me, too," Susannah agreed, laughing. "When I was a kid back in Zach's Corners, it was my favorite dessert."

"You're from Zach's Corners?" Marianne exclaimed. "So are we. Jake and I were born there. We—" She stopped and stared. "Oh, my gosh. Now I know why you look so familiar," she said in a tight voice. "You're a Dushay, aren't you?"

The shock Susannah felt on hearing that Jake was from her hometown was quickly replaced by a feeling of dread. He had deliberately kept that bit of information from her. Why?

"Yes," she replied absently, her gaze seeking her husband. She found herself the object of his intense stare. "Jake, why didn't you—?"

"We'll talk about it later, Susannah. Why don't you go get the pie now? And make a pot of coffee, too." His voice was low but commanding, and Susannah did not even consider arguing, sensing that her questions would be best asked in private.

Jake's brooding gaze followed Susannah when she excused herself and went into the kitchen. The instant the door swung closed behind her the other two at the table pounced, as he'd known they would.

"Dammit, Jake!" Grant exploded in a gritty undertone. "Have you lost your mind?"

"She's Philip's sister, isn't she?"

"His half sister." Ignoring Grant's outburst, he met Marianne's accusing look head-on.

"Jake, what's going on here?"

"Don't you see what he's up to, darling?" Grant put in furiously. "He's using that girl to get revenge on the Dushays."

Marianne's eyes widened. "Is that true? Are you?"

Jake's gaze never wavered. "Can you think of a better way? Imagine how Nathan's going to feel when he finds out his daughter has married a Taggart."

"Oh, Jake," Marianne said with infinite sadness. "Why can't you just let it go? I have. It all happened so long ago. We've built new lives. Better lives. Striking back at Nathan and Philip won't accomplish anything. Hatred and revenge will only rebound on you."

"It'll give me satisfaction," Jake said in a steel-edged voice. "Don't you understand? It's not just what they did to you. It's all of it—running us out of town, robbing us of our livelihood and our dignity, practically stealing our land, which was the only thing of any value we had."

"I know, but—"

"Dammit, Marianne. If Nathan hadn't forced Pop to sell our land our father wouldn't have had the money to buy that old junker of a car he wrapped around that utility pole. It took the fire department four hours just to cut our mother's body out of that mangled mess. Remember? What I'm doing to Nathan is little enough misery for what he's caused us."

"And what about Susannah? She seems like a nice person. Does she deserve to be hurt this way? You have to know that she will be when she finds out why you married her."

"Marianne's right," Grant said. "Susannah isn't to blame. Hell, she was just a child when it happened."

Some of the cold fury went out of Jake's eyes, and he looked down at his fingers, idly turning his water glass. "I never wanted to harm her, but it can't be helped. I've got to hit Nathan and Philip where it hurts—in the gut. My only chance of doing that is through Susannah."

"I see. So what happens to her after you've gotten your revenge? Will you just dump her?"

"Of course not. She's my wife. She'll remain my wife."

"Oh, Jake." Marianne shook her head sadly. "Do you honestly think she'll want to stay in this marriage once she knows the truth? It would take a powerful love to survive a blow like the one you're going to deal her."

Jake's teeth clenched tighter. The mere thought of Susannah leaving him brought a suffocating feeling. The fact that it did made him even more uneasy. Dammit! He didn't want to think about the aftermath. Not yet.

He shrugged, carefully keeping his expression closed. "It's her choice, of course. She's free to stay or go as she pleases, but whatever happens, I'll deal with it. In the meantime, you two are to say nothing to Susannah about this. Understand?"

"Hell, man, she's going to find out sooner or later," Grant argued.

"When we meet with her family will be soon enough."

"And when will that be?" Marianne watched him with a troubled expression. "You've been married five weeks. I'm amazed you haven't already confronted Nathan and Philip."

He shot his sister an annoyed look. He didn't like being reminded of the number of times he'd put off the showdown with the Dushays. "I haven't had time. I've been busy lately."

"Too busy to make a two-hour drive?"

"Yes," he replied testily. "Now can we drop it? I'll attend to the matter soon. Until then, there's no reason for Susannah to be upset."

Both Marianne and Grant looked ready to say more, but Susannah, bearing a tray, pushed through the swinging door.

"Here we go. Coffee and rhubarb pie," she said as cheerfully as she could manage.

The instant Susannah entered the room she became aware of the strained atmosphere. Jake's expression was unreadable, but Marianne and Grant looked grim. The gaiety and excitement her sister-in-law had exhibited during the meal had vanished. Her expression polite but remote, Marianne nibbled at her pie in silence and barely glanced Susannah's way.

The minute they finished dessert the Calloways announced that they had to leave. Marianne made a perfunctory offer to help with the dishes but Susannah refused; she could not take one more minute of the uncomfortable silence that had marked the last part of the meal.

"Why didn't you tell me you were from Zach's Corners?" Susannah asked Jake when they had gone. She stood in the doorway, facing him across the width of the living room, feeling frightened and shaky and unsure of what to expect.

Jake bent over and plucked a mint from the dish on the coffee table. He popped the candy in his mouth and rolled it on his tongue, studying her. "When you lived in Zach's Corners did you ever hear of The Swamp?"

"The Swamp?" Susannah frowned. "You mean that trashy river bottom area south of town?"

A tiny, cold smile curved Jake's mouth. "You got it. Where the town's have-nots and undesirables live. Zach's Corners' version of the wrong side of the tracks, only in this case it's the wrong side of the river." He paused, watching her. "That's where the Taggarts lived, in a shanty pieced together out of scrap wood and tar paper. My father was the town drunk, and my mother worked as a maid in your house."

The information surprised Susannah but it wasn't what she wanted to know. "You still haven't answered my question."

"I didn't tell you because I figured if you remembered who I was you wouldn't have anything to do with me."

It took a minute for his meaning to soak in. When it did, Susannah felt a sharp tug on her heart.

Her expression softened. "Oh, Jake." Emotion clogged her throat, and her voice came out a quavering whisper. "How could you think that any of that would matter to me? I don't care if you were raised in The Swamp or a palace. I love you."

She hurried across the room and wrapped her arms around his waist. Hugging him with all her might, she snuggled her face against his chest and squeezed her eyes shut. It had never occurred to her that Jake, her tough, determined, self-assured husband, might be insecure about his origins. It was the first chink she had discovered in his armor, and while she never wanted him to suffer a moment's doubt about her love, nevertheless, it gave her hope.

Jake returned the fierce embrace, his expression pained. Guilt stabbed at him. He hadn't lied...exactly. If Susannah had known all there was to know about him she would have shunned him. All right, so he'd known she would misinterpret his statement. He was just trying to protect her for as long as he could.

"I love you, Jake," Susannah repeated in a fierce whisper, squeezing him tighter. "I always will."

He grasped her shoulders and held her away from him, studying her so intently that she shivered. "Will you, baby?" he said deeply.

"Yes. Always."

The words were mere wisps of sound, quavery with emotion. He watched her, saw her eyes soften with love, watched the entrancing color rise in her cheeks. He felt his own body warm, and the urgent heaviness pool in his loins.

She gasped and clutched at his shoulders when he swept her up in his arms and strode from the room. "Ja-aake! Where are you taking me?"

"To bed."

"But the dishes—"

"Can wait. This can't."

He caught her mouth in a kiss of such deliberate intimacy that she went weak, and with a sigh she curled in his arms.

After a night of passion, so fantastic that for days afterward she would blush whenever she thought of it, Susannah awoke the next morning feeling on top of the world, and her mood only improved when, over breakfast, Jake suggested that she start house hunting.

Surprised, Susannah stared at him, hardly daring to believe she had heard him right. "Are you serious? You really want us to move into a house?"

Jake shrugged. "This apartment was okay when I was a bachelor, but it doesn't feel much like a home. Aside from that, a house is a good investment. But perhaps I'm taking too much for granted. I just assumed that you'd prefer a house."

"I would! Really! You just took me by surprise is all."

"In that case, why don't you get started looking right away? You've got a little time before school starts." Jake wiped his mouth with a napkin and stood up.

Susannah followed him to the door, almost skipping around him in excitement while he slipped into his suit coat and retrieved his briefcase, bombarding him with questions about the kind of house he wanted, neighborhoods he preferred, price range, size and a myriad of other things. Most, he answered, but finally, in frustration he said, "Look, why don't you just take Marianne with you? She knows all that and she enjoys looking at houses. Plus, it'll give you two a chance to get acquainted."

Susannah knew a good suggestion when she heard one. The only problem was, she ran into resistance from Marianne. The first day she telephoned, her sister-in-law pleaded jet lag, the next a previous engagement, the next a headache.

The fourth day Susannah didn't risk a polite refusal over the telephone. She looked up the Calloways' address in Jake's directory and drove to their house.

Surprised dismay flashed in her sister-in-law's face when she answered the door. She quickly masked her feelings and invited Susannah inside, but not before Susannah had seen the reaction. She knew then that she had not imagined the standoffish tone in Marianne's voice when they'd talked over the telephone.

With a stiff smile, Marianne offered coffee, but Susannah declined and got straight to the point. As before, the request was barely out of her mouth when Marianne started to refuse, but she didn't give her the chance.

"Please, Marianne," she pleaded. "I desperately need your help. Jake is counting on me and I haven't a clue of what to look for, or even where to start."

"Susannah..." Marianne hesitated and bit her lower lip. As Susannah had hoped, refusing a request face-to-face was much more difficult than doing so over the telephone. "I really don't—"

"Please, don't say no. Jake said you've done this before and you knew all about dealing with a Realtor. I've never even spoken to one. Please, Marianne. Help me."

Marianne looked skeptical. "Are you sure Jake is serious about this? I mean...he's never been even remotely interested in owning a house before."

"It was his suggestion."

Susannah looked at her hopefully, and after a while Marianne sighed. "All right. I'll go."

On the drive to the Realtor's office Marianne remained detached, but Susannah didn't let it discourage her. She knew that underneath that cool facade her sister-in-law was a warm, outgoing person, and she was determined to win her over.

Since Marianne had been friendly until she discovered that Susannah was a Dushay, she had a hunch what the problem was, and she wasted no time setting things straight.

"Jake explained everything to me after you and Grant left the other night," she mentioned casually, breaking the strained silence that filled the car.

Marianne's head snapped around. She stared at Susannah, her face shocked. "He *told* you? And you're not angry?"

"Of course not. It doesn't matter to me that your family lived in The Swamp. I'm not a snob, Marianne," she chastised gently, slanting her a reproving look. "Not that I blame you for assuming so—I can't deny that my father and brother are impossibly class-conscious. But I wasn't brought up to think that way. What you don't know is Mother divorced my father when I was ten. For the past seventeen years she and I have lived in a modest duplex on Houston's east side. So you see, you have no reason to feel uncomfortable or resentful around me."

"I see," Marianne said in a subdued voice. "You're right, of course. I apologize for misjudging you. It was rude of me."

"That's all right, I understand." Susannah took her eyes off the road long enough to send Marianne a warm smile. "I would like very much for us to be friends."

In silence, Marianne searched her face, and for a brief instant her intensity reminded Susannah sharply of Jake. Finally, her expression softened and her mouth curved in a faint, if somewhat resigned, smile. "Of course."

Marianne warned Susannah that finding the right house often took weeks, even months, of legwork, and not to be too disappointed if they didn't find anything right away.

That morning they looked at numerous houses in River Oaks and Memorial, two posh neighborhoods close to the Jetco Building. Within the price range that Jake had given her—which made her gulp whenever she thought about it—there had been several gorgeous places to choose from, but nothing really struck a chord with Susannah, until they walked into an elegant but homey old farmhouse on the far northwest side of town.

At one time it had been out in the country, surrounded by several thousand acres of farm land, but the steady encroachment of the city had put it at the edge of town. Rising taxes and diminishing profits to farmers had whittled away at the family's holding until now all that was left was the house and the eighty acres surrounding it.

When they drove up the long tree-lined drive and saw the stately old clapboard house nestled in a stand of ancient oaks, Susannah was enchanted. The minute she walked through the front door she was in love.

Rushing from room to room, she felt like an excited child at Christmas. She exclaimed over the wooden floors, the hand-carved banisters, the fancy moldings and generous-size rooms.

"I take it you like this one," Marianne said with a laugh.

"Like it? I love it!" Susannah was so excited she felt like twirling on her toes like a child. She darted about so fast, Marianne could barely keep up with her.

But when she entered the small room adjacent to the master bedroom on the second floor, she came to a halt and gazed at the sunny yellow-and-white room, entranced. "Oh, look, Marianne," she whispered with awe. "It's a nursery."

"Yes. So I see." But it was Susannah's face, not the room that her sister-in-law was studying. "From the look on your face, I gather that you would like to have a family."

"Oh, yes," Susannah said dreamily. "I'd like that very much."

"Have, uh . . . have you talked to Jake about it?"

"Not yet. But I will." Just thinking about the possibility made Susannah tremble. If her calculations were correct, she and Jake might be having that conversation soon. The temptation to tell Marianne of her suspicion was strong, but Susannah held back. She was, after all, only a few days late, and she had always been horribly irregular. She could be getting her hopes up over nothing.

Susannah felt Marianne's stare, and she turned to find her sister-in-law studying her, a frown creasing her brow. "Good heavens. You're positively glowing," she said in a slightly appalled voice. "You're really serious about this, aren't you?"

"Very serious," Susannah replied with heartfelt emotion. "I can't think of anything more wonderful than having Jake's babies."

Marianne stared, her eyes growing wide with dawning comprehension.

The door to Jake's office burst open, and he looked up from the contract he was reading to see his sister storm inside with fire in her eyes.

"I want to talk to you, Jake Taggart. Right now!"

Tossing his pencil on the desk, he leaned back in his chair and fixed Marianne with a look of amused indulgence. "All right. Fire away."

"For starters, I ought to wring your neck for siccing Susannah on me."

Jake sobered instantly. "Sorry, I thought, if you gave it a chance, you just might like her."

"Of course I like her!" Marianne practically shouted, pacing before the desk. "I didn't expect to. I even tried hard not to. But it didn't work. Who could *not* like Susannah? She's sweet and unaffected and genuinely nice, for goodness' sake!''

"Yes, Susannah is very likable," he agreed with a trace of his former humor. "So what's the problem?"

Heaving a sigh, Marianne sank down in one of the chairs before his desk, her ire fizzling into sadness. "The problem is she loves you, Jake," she said forlornly. "I thought at first that she might have married you for your money, but her feelings are written all over her face whenever she talks about you. She truly loves you."

Jake's jaw set. "I know."

"Do you love her at all?" Marianne asked quietly.

"I . . . care about her."

"Then, in heaven's name, how can you hurt her this way?"

Her questions were like roweling spurs on his already sore conscience. For weeks, similar thoughts had been bedeviling him. Daily, the struggle to subdue them was becoming more and more difficult. "What you don't seem to realize is, even if I wanted to change my mind, it's too late. Susannah and I are married. Nathan is going to learn about it eventually."

"Then at least tell her yourself. Now, while you still might salvage something out of this. Don't let it come as a shock to her in front of Nathan and Philip. She'll still be hurt, of course, but if you explain to Susannah what happened and how you felt, she'll understand."

Jake stared at his sister, his expression unchanged. He knew she was right. Susannah was the most giving and forgiving person he'd ever known. It went against the grain, though, to bare his soul. He didn't like explaining his actions. Not to anyone.

"I'll think about it."

"But—"

"Leave it alone, Marianne," he said in a steely voice.

Her shoulders sagged. "Just tell me one thing. If you're so set on seeing this through to the bitter end, why are you putting Susannah through this charade of buying a house? She's running around with stars in her eyes thinking about filling a nursery with babies, for heaven's sake!"

Something hot and sweet seemed to explode in Jake's chest. The thought of Susannah carrying his child was unbearably tempting. It pulled at him. *She* pulled at him, in a way he'd never experienced before. She was occupying his thoughts more and more, blurring the sharp edges of pain and bitterness. Sometimes, days went by without his recalling the reason she was in his life. And now, to make things worse, the picture of a child suckling at her breast stamped itself on his mind.

Gritting his teeth, Jake thrust the image away violently. Dammit! He could not let those kinds of feelings get in his way. Not now, when he was this close.

"I have my reasons. That's all you need to know."

Marianne made a disgusted sound and stood up. "Grant is right. You are, without doubt, the most secretive, stubborn, *pigheaded* man."

"Marianne," Jake said quietly, stopping her before she reached the door. She looked at him over her shoulder, one eyebrow cocked in impatient inquiry. "Make sure that Susannah picks a house she really likes."

Her eyes slowly widened. "Oh, my Lord. You're buying this house for her as some sort of consolation, aren't you?"

Jake simply looked at her.

By mid-August the house was theirs. Susannah had no idea how Jake managed it, but somehow he rushed the paperwork through, and two weeks after she found the house they closed the deal. To celebrate, they were having dinner that evening at the Calloways', but since Jake had a late appointment and Susannah planned to go to their new home and take some measurements, they agreed to meet at his sister's.

That evening, Susannah rang the Calloways' doorbell feeling on top of the world. She couldn't remember ever being so happy. When Marianne opened the door, she beamed at her. "Hi. I see that Jake beat me here," she said gaily, motioning toward the silver Porsche in the driveway.

"Uh...yes, he's here." Marianne bit her lip and glanced back over her shoulder, hesitating briefly before stepping back and opening the door wide. "Come in."

"Marianne? Is something wrong?" Susannah asked, noticing the nervous glances she was receiving.

"No. It's just that...well, my son came home unexpectedly. He got here just a few minutes ago."

"Seth! Oh, how great!" She slipped her arm through Marianne's and urged her toward the living room. "Well, come on. I can't wait to meet him."

When they stepped into the room, the gangly youth sprawled on the sofa sprang to his feet and came toward her with his hand outstretched. "Hi! You must be Uncle Jake's wife. I'm Seth."

Of their own accord, Susannah's feet stopped working. She stood rooted to a spot a few feet inside the door, suddenly unable to breathe, her heart galloping at a sickening pace. She was only marginally aware of Jake, standing motionless on the other side of the room, watching her, or of Grant, trying discreetly not to. Her attention was centered on the teenage boy with the silvery blond hair and green eyes who took her limp hand and pumped it vigorously.

"I knew you'd be something, for Uncle Jake to take the plunge. I didn't think he'd ever get married," he said with a broad grin that revealed a full set of metal braces. "Hey! You know something? I kinda look like you."

"N-no." Susannah's voice came out wobbly and pain filled, barely above a whisper. "You look exactly like my brother."

Chapter Ten

"No kidding? Hey, that's wild." Seth's grin stretched wider. "People'll probably think you're my real aunt. I mean...you know...instead of just by marriage."

Susannah's throat was so tight she couldn't reply. The pain of betrayal nearly buckled her knees. One by one, her wounded gaze sought out the other three people in the room. Marianne and Grant were barely able to meet her eyes, but Jake watched her with his usual intensity. When she encountered that unwavering gray-eyed stare, her fragile composure shattered.

"I...I can't—" Her chin wobbled. She fought back a sob, and then another, her upper body jerking with the effort. She looked at them through a blur of tears and moved her head from side to side. "I ca-can't stay here. I...can't."

The last came out on a broken sob as she turned and ran.

"Susannah! Susannah, come back here!" Jake bellowed, but she paid him no mind. Biting off a vicious curse, he took off after her. Three steps away he collided with Seth, who was scrambling to get out of his path.

"Oh, for Pete's sake!" After a fruitless effort to dodge the gangly boy, Jake grasped his shoulders, moved him aside, and dashed out of the room.

"Jake, don't let her leave like this! Stop her!" Marianne called needlessly after him.

"Hey! What's going on? What'd I say?"

Vaguely, from behind him, Jake heard Seth's bewildered questions, but his mind was on Susannah. He heard the squeal of rubber on pavement and bolted through the front door in time to see her car shoot down the curving U-shaped drive and bump out onto the street without slowing, the rear end of the vehicle fishtailing and tires screaming as she took the turn. He stood helplessly on the lawn, watching the red glow of taillights disappear around the corner. "Damn!"

Like a wounded animal, Susannah instinctively headed for the one person she knew she could trust: Marta. Without being aware of doing so, or how she managed it, she drove straight to the run-down little duplex, and there she threw herself into her old friend's comforting arms and sobbed out the awful story.

"How could he do this?" she cried against Marta's motherly bosom. "How could he?"

Marta sighed and patted Susannah's heaving shoulders. "I know it hurts, child, but what you have to keep in mind is that it's part of Jake's nature to strike back when he's been wronged. I'm not saying it's right, just that it's instinct to him."

"Wh-what am I going to d-do, Marta? I know it's cr-crazy, but I still l-love him," she wailed piteously.

"Then you go home and you wait and hope. Remember, a Scorpio can choose his path in life. He can emulate the vengeful, stinging scorpion, or he can transform himself into an eagle and soar above that kind of bitterness. The magical power of Pluto is always there for him. All he has to do is call on it." Marta lifted Susannah's tear-streaked face and smiled encouragingly. "You have to trust him to make the right choice. If he loves you, he will."

Jake was waiting for her when she reached the apartment. The moment she stepped into the foyer, he appeared in the living room doorway. He studied her in that disconcerting direct way of his, his face dark and brooding. "We have to talk."

Susannah lifted her chin and, without a word, walked past him into the living room. She sat on the sofa and folded her hands together in her lap. Jake stood before the fireplace, his hands in his pockets, his somber gaze locked on her.

"Are you all right?"

"I'm fine." She felt fragile, brittle almost, as though she would shatter into a million pieces at any moment, but she would not let him see that.

"Where have you been?"

"Marta's."

Jake winced at the succinct reply, and Susannah felt a dart of satisfaction. Oddly, Jake and Marta had become good friends, and she knew he regretted damaging the relationship.

"I was going to tell you," he said quietly.

Susannah's head snapped up, her eyes flashing. "Oh, really? When? As we were turning into my father's driveway?"

"Tonight, after we got home." She gave a derisive little snort, which Jake ignored. "Are you ready to hear about it now?" he asked quietly.

"I suppose."

"Marianne was just sixteen that summer," he began. "Sixteen and starry-eyed." Slowly, bluntly, Jake told her everything that had happened seventeen years before. He also told her about his parents' deaths, two years after her father had forced them out of town, and about his own long, determined struggle to achieve financial success.

"I learned that summer that success and wealth translate to power. The day I left Zach's Corners I made up my mind that I was going to have both. Everything I've done since then, all the work, the study, the effort, has been for one purpose."

"Revenge," Susannah murmured, looking at him with a mixture of horror and pity. "Since that's your goal, I'm surprised that you haven't tried to ruin my father financially."

"I thought about it. A lot. But then I realized that was too easy. Besides, that's only money. I wanted to hit him where it hurt."

"So, you married me, knowing he would hate it." Hurt and disillusionment quavered in her voice. "I suppose I should count myself lucky that you didn't just seduce me like Philip—" She looked up, her words faltering when she saw something flicker in his hard stare. "Oh . . . I see. That was your original intention, wasn't it?" she said with commendable aplomb, considering the pain that stabbed at her.

"Yes. But I couldn't go through with it."

"My, how noble of you." Susannah gave a bitter little laugh. "The funny thing is, it would have worked. I was so blinded by love I would have done anything you wanted."

Jake looked at her steadily. "I know."

Scalding heat washed over Susannah's face and neck, and she lowered her gaze, humiliated almost to the point of tears. She stared at her intertwined fingers. "So . . . what happens now?"

"That depends on you. Now that you know everything, what are you going to do?"

Reflexively, Susannah pressed her palm against her lower abdomen, and the child she was almost sure nestled there. Pride urged her to leave, but she wasn't sure she could bear to. No matter what Jake had done, she couldn't deprive him of his child. And the simple truth was, though crushed and heartsick, she still loved him.

She raised her head and looked at him, praying for some sign of affection, some reason to hope, but in his eyes she saw only hard, unrelenting determination. "I...I don't know."

He continued to regard her in silence, his expression unchanged. Then, finally, he announced, "In that case, there's no point in delaying any longer. We'll leave for Zach's Corners in the morning."

Jake gritted his teeth when Susannah's head snapped up and he saw the pain in her eyes. He wanted to go to her, fold her in his arms and make everything right, but it was too late. As he watched, she averted her gaze and drew herself up proudly, pulling her composure around her like a cloak.

"Very well," she said tonelessly, and stood up. Holding herself stiffly, her face paper white, she walked out of the room.

Jake brought the car to a halt in the driveway. He sat motionless and stared at the red brick mansion, his hands still clenched around the steering wheel. The last time he'd been there he'd been thrown out of the house like so much garbage. Anticipation tightened his chest. He didn't expect his reception would be any more congenial this time, but he was sure as hell going to enjoy it more.

He glanced at Susannah's strained face and frowned, his eagerness fading. She looked as fragile as fine crystal. During the two-hour drive she'd barely said a word.

Jake's jaw clenched, and he reached for the door handle. "Let's go."

The elderly housekeeper greeted Susannah with affection and eyed Jake curiously, then showed them into the parlor and went to inform her father of their arrival. While Susannah wandered over to the French doors that looked out on the side garden, Jake watched her, worry gnawing at him.

"Susannah! What in heaven's name are you doing here at this hour?"

Nathan stomped into the room with an impatient scowl on his face, and Philip strolled in after him. Neither man saw Jake, standing to one side, watching the scene unfold.

In seventeen years both men had put on weight. In the son it had taken the form of a thickening waist and the beginnings of a double chin, which, Jake had no doubt, would eventually develop into fleshy jowls like those that hung over his father's collar. Nathan's hair was now more silver than blond, and the beefiness of seventeen years ago had become a paunch. Philip had the appearance of an aging playboy, his once handsome face sagging with lines of dissipation and set in a sulky look of boredom.

Susannah turned from the window, her expression carefully polite, her eyes wary. "Hello, Father. Philip."

Neither man made a move to embrace her, or to even get within touching distance. Noting the omission, Jake frowned.

An attractive but cowed-looking dark-haired woman of about thrity-five slipped into the room and stood just inside the doorway. Susannah's gaze flickered to her. "Hello, Elaine."

Nathan shot the woman an annoyed glance, then turned his attention back to Susannah. "Well, girl? I assume there is a reason for this surprise visit, so out with it. Your brother and I were just about to leave for the mill."

"I came to tell you that I got married," she replied in a wooden voice. "And to introduce you to my husband. This is Jake Taggart."

"Married!"

"Did you say Taggart?"

Both men spoke at once, their startled gazes swinging to where Jake stood beside the grand piano.

"Hello, Nathan." Jake's hard stare drilled the older man for several seconds, then switched to his son. "Philip. Ah, I see that you remember me. How's the nose?"

"My God," Philip gasped. His bored expression vanished, and he gaped at Jake.

"Taggart? Taggart?" Nathan's eyes suddenly widened in recognition, then narrowed. "You're one of the bunch I ran out of town years ago, aren't you? The one I threw out of here?"

"The same." Jake leaned back against the piano and crossed his arms over his chest. "But if I were you, I wouldn't try it again."

"Oh? And why not? You think because you somehow got this foolish daughter of mine to marry you that I can't toss you out of here? Think again, Swamp trash."

"Father!"

Both men ignored Susannah's shocked cry.

"I didn't say you *couldn't* try," Jake said in a soft, deadly voice. "I just don't advise it."

Nathan's bushy brows rose at the subtle threat. Jake's unflinching control and steely stare gave him pause.

"Amos and Billy are working out back in the stables, Father," Philip volunteered nervously. "Shall I call them in?"

"No, son. We can handle this. It won't take long." Nathan looked Jake over, a derisive smile twitching his mouth. "You think a suit and a shoe shine changes what you are, Taggart? Hell, you can dress a pig in sequins, but it's still a pig."

"Father, stop it!"

Nathan turned scornful eyes on Susannah. "And as for you, you're as silly and stupid as that mother of yours was. She didn't have the breeding or discrimination to fit in among people of our class, and apparently, neither do you, or you wouldn't have soiled yourself with this trash."

Susannah flinched at the harsh words, and Jake straightened away from the piano, his body tensing. "Watch it, Dushay. No one talks to my wife that way. Not even her father."

"Ah, yes. By all means, leap to her defense. After all, she's your passport to a better life, isn't she? You must keep her happy and convince her you really care."

"That's not true!" Susannah cried.

"Don't be stupid, girl," Nathan snapped with real venom. "You can't possibly believe that he married you because he loves you." Susannah's stricken look brought a smile to his lips. "There, you see, even you are smart enough to figure that out. The only reason he married you was to get his hands on my money and to try to better his social position."

Nathan turned back to Jake with malicious delight. "Too bad, Taggart. It won't work. Susannah won't be receiving one red cent from me. I cut her out of my will years ago. If she wants to squander her life on the likes of you, I really don't care. As far as I'm concerned, she ceased to be my true daughter when she left here with her mother."

Susannah gave a little cry and swayed, her face going chalky white. Jake crossed the room in three long strides and slipped his arm around her waist.

He looked at Nathan with cold fury in his eyes. He wanted to break the man in two with his bare hands for what he was doing to Susannah. "You bastard."

Nathan smiled back, unperturbed. "Your show of touching concern is wasted, boy. Face it, you gambled and lost. When are you Taggarts going to learn not to tangle with your betters?"

Philip snickered, emboldened by his father's arrogance, but the sound was cut off by a killing look from Jake. He had a fierce need to plant his fist in the little weasel's face and break his nose for him again, but his concern for Susannah was greater.

She held herself stiffly, trying desperately to hold on to her pride and keep from falling apart, but he could feel the violent tremors from within that shook her whole body. He looked down at her white face and wounded eyes and felt her pain all the way to his soul.

His arm tightened around her. "Come on, sweetheart. Let's get out of here."

"An excellent idea," Nathan drawled. "Philip will show you out."

"Don't bother." Jake's gaze speared Susannah's half brother, warning him not to come anywhere near her. Keeping Susannah clamped against his side, Jake solicitously guided her out of the room, through the foyer, past the hand-wringing housekeeper, who had apparently heard every word, and out the front door. Susannah obeyed his urgings without question or hesitation, moving in a pain-filled daze with the stiff, jerky steps of a robot. They reached the car, and Jake started to hand Susannah inside when Philip called to him in a low voice.

"Taggart! Psst! Taggart, wait up."

Surprised, Jake turned and saw him ease out the door. He paused, his eyes darting furtively around, then hurried down the steps to where Jake stood protectively over Susannah. "What do you want, Philip?"

"Take it easy. I just want a little information." He rubbed his palms together nervously and looked around again, then lowered his voice. "I just thought you could tell me...you know...what Marianne had, a boy or a girl. Hey! I gotta right to know," he protested when Jake's expression turned menacing. "It's my kid."

"Why you—" Jake started to go after him, but Susannah clung to his arm and held him back.

"Jake, don't!" She looked at her half brother. "No, it isn't, Philip. You forfeited all claim to that child long ago."

"So, what did she do? Give the kid up for adoption?"

Jake tensed, ready to hit him, but Susannah's fingers dug into the tight muscles in his forearm. He looked down and saw the warning in her eyes and stilled. "Yes," she replied in an unemotional voice. "The child has been adopted."

She turned away, dismissing Philip without a backward glance and looked at Jake beseechingly. "Can we go now, please?"

In her eyes he saw how much the confrontation had cost her and he knew that she was holding on to her composure by a thread. Without a word, he bundled her into the Porsche and hurried around to the other side.

Halfway down the hill, Jake glanced at Susannah. She sat ramrod stiff, staring straight ahead, her hands clenched so tight her knuckles were white.

"You okay?"

She pressed her lips together and nodded.

"What was that all about back there? Why did you lie to Philip?"

"I didn't lie. You told me yourself that Grant adopted Seth. Anyway, believe me, it's best that Philip think he's out of reach. He and Elaine are childless after twelve years of marriage, and Philip is getting desperate for a son. I wouldn't put it past him to try to take Seth if he knew where to find him."

"I'd see him in hell first," Jake ground out. His hands clenched the steering wheel as if it were Philip Dushay's neck, and his jaw set. He was so occupied with his furious thoughts, they were out of town before he glanced at Susannah again. What he saw made him wince.

She trembled from head to foot, as though in the grip of a hard chill. Silent tears streamed down her colorless cheeks and dripped, unheeded, from her chin, spotting the front of her dress and splattering her clenched hands. Jake had never seen such abject misery and pain in his life.

"Hey, honey, come on. Don't cry like that. Those two aren't worth it," he coaxed, but she didn't seem to hear him. She stared straight ahead, her despair all-consuming.

Jake stomped on the gas and sent the Porsche streaking down the highway like a launched rocket. Ten minutes later, he brought the car to a screeching halt in the parking lot of a small motel on the outskirts of the next town. As he hurriedly registered, he kept an eye on Susannah through the office window, but she simply sat there motionless, her silent tears still flowing. Jake doubted that she even knew he had stopped.

He parked the Porsche directly in front of their room, unlocked the door, then lifted her from the car and carried her inside. Susannah neither helped nor hindered, but curled docilely in his arms and continued to weep. Murmuring to her constantly, Jake undressed her and tucked her into bed, then quickly stripped and slid in beside her, wrapping his arms around her, pulling her close into his heat.

"Shh. Don't cry, baby. Come on. You're going to make yourself sick. He's not worth one of your tears." Jake rubbed his hands up and down her slender back, trying to take away the pain her father had so cruelly inflicted. "Come on, love. Let it go. I can't stand to see you hurting like this."

The crooned words, instead of calming, made her cry harder, her sobs breaking loose, the raw sounds filling the room. Hot tears dripped into the hair on Jake's chest, plastering the tight curls against his skin. Grimacing, he tightened his hold and stroked her. Her pathetic weeping made him feel murderous. If Nathan Dushay had been within reach he would have strangled him.

It was then that Jake realized that he loved Susannah. It hit him like a fist to the heart, stunning him momentarily, then filling him with pain as he accepted blame for his part in inflicting this agony on her.

He held Susannah close and stared across the cheap motel room. Had he loved her when he proposed? Probably, he admitted. Which explained why he'd put off today's confrontation for so long. Oh, there had been a string of excuses: his workload, a meeting with an important customer, a labor dispute, an accident at the plant. All were legitimate, but none so urgent that he couldn't have taken one day to drive to Zach's Corners. The plain truth that he had refused to accept was he enjoyed being married to Susannah. The past couple of months he'd been happier and more content than he could remember ever being, and he supposed, subconsciously, he hadn't wanted to rock the boat.

Susannah stirred, and Jake whispered comforting words in her ear. Gradually her tears began to taper off. He kept holding her, stroking her back and hips, murmuring to her gently, and after a while she began to relax in his arms. She nestled close, releasing a shuddering sigh, and he felt the hair on his chest stir, the moist warmth of her breath feather over his skin.

For a long while they lay quietly. From outside came the whine of cars zooming by on the highway, the occasional rumble of an eighteen-wheeler. Inside, the only sounds were the drip of a faucet in the bathroom and the soft sibilance of their breathing. She lay warm against him, her body soft in all the right places. With every breath he inhaled the clean scent of her hair and that intoxicating woman fragrance that was hers alone. A shaft of morning sunshine stabbed through a crack in the curtains like a tiny spotlight. Jake watched the dust motes floating in the golden beam, part of him wishing the tranquil moment would never end.

"Ja-Jake?"

His hand glided from the base of Susannah's spine up to her neck. "Hmm?"

"I . . . I'm sorry for falling to pieces like that."

"Hey!" He pulled back and tipped her face up. Her eyes were red and swollen, the lashes spiked. Tears still glistened on her cheeks and her whole face was puffy and blotched from the bout of weeping. Yet never had she looked more beautiful to him. "You don't have anything to apologize for. You're entitled to cry, although I personally don't think your father is worth grieving over."

Her chin wobbled, and she blinked rapidly as fresh tears threatened. "We were never close. Not even when I lived at home," she confessed in an aching little voice that twisted Jake's heart. "Since the divorce, we've grown apart even further. You expect a parent to love you, no matter what, but I suppose, deep down, I always knew he didn't. But suspecting is one thing, and hearing it said is...is..."

"Shh." Jake folded her close again and rocked her. "I know it hurts, babe. But you don't need his love. You have mine."

He felt her stiffen and go absolutely still, and his heart clenched. Sweat broke out on his forehead. Had he destroyed her love for him? He swallowed hard and gathered his courage. "Did you hear me, Susannah? I said I love you."

"Jake, please...don't."

Pain slashed through him, and he squeezed his eyes shut. "Don't what?" he asked when he'd caught his breath. "Don't love you? Don't say it? Don't even think it? What?"

"Don't pretend. I don't want your pity."

"Pity!" He pulled away again and forced her to look at him. Her expression was oddly mulish and vulnerable all at the same time, her soft green eyes awash with resentment and pain. "Is that what you think? That I'm just feeling sorry for you?"

"You know how much my father hurt me and you're trying to make me feel better. Well, it isn't necessary. I'll get over it on my own. I don't need or want your lies."

Until that moment, he hadn't known that you could feel anger and elation at the same time. Holding her face clamped in the V between his thumb and fingers, he stared deep into her eyes. "Listen to me, Susannah Taggart," he said in a deep, raspy voice that made her shiver. "Yes, I feel bad about what your father said to you. I also feel partly responsible. But I've felt sympathetic toward other women before and I sure as hell never told one that I loved her. So listen to me, honey, and listen good. I love you. More than I can say. More than I ever imagined loving anyone. And I expect to go on loving you until the day I die. Is that clear enough for you?"

Wide-eyed, Susannah searched his face, afraid to hope and helpless not to. From somewhere in the recesses of her mind came snippets of the sorts of things Marta had said. *A Scorpio is bluntly honest.... You can be sure he means every word he says.... His natural intensity makes him capable of loving deeply....*

Susannah's heart speeded up. She licked her lips. "Oh, Jake," she said unsteadily. "Are you sure? Really sure? Because if you change your mind I couldn't stand—"

He stopped the flow of anguished words with a hard kiss. When at last he pulled back, he gave her a look so intense Susannah could barely breathe. "Yes, I'm sure. I've never been more sure of anything in my life. I love you, Susannah." He stroked a curl away from her temple, and his devouring gaze roamed over her face. "Sweet heaven, how I love you," he whispered.

"Oh, Jake." Her eyes filled with tears, which then spilled over onto her cheeks. With a glad cry, she looped her arms around his neck, buried her face against his shoulder and sobbed.

"Oh, Lord, not again. I thought you'd be happy."

"I...I am ha...hap...py. That's why I'm cr-crying," she wailed.

Jake groaned and wrapped his arms around her. Confused and feeling utterly helpless, he held her close as she gave in to the storm of emotion. He rocked her gently and let her cry it out, his hands moving over her hair, her back, her shoulders in slow, smooth strokes.

Finally her tears stopped and she sniffled.

"Jake?" she said tentatively after a moment, her face still buried against his neck.

"Hmm?"

"Where are we?"

"In a motel."

"Why?"

"You were upset and needed comforting. This seemed like the best place for it."

"But . . . we're naked."

Jake raised up on one elbow and gave her a long, heated look. "Yes," he said deeply, and smiled as he watched her pupils widen and her green eyes go soft and hazy with passion.

Chapter Eleven

The reality of being loved by Jake far exceeded all of Susannah's dreams. Toward the rest of the world, he remained distant, hiding his feelings and thoughts behind an inscrutable expression and a searing look that kept all but the bravest at arm's length. He loved his sister and nephew, and with them and a few close friends like Grant and Alice, he was more relaxed and open, but only with Susannah did all his defenses come down.

With her he was loving and warm. In the privacy of their bedroom, as they lay wrapped in each other's arms, he poured out his deepest thoughts and hopes and fears, things she was sure he had never shared with another living being. It was as though, in loving her, he had given her the key to not only his heart, but his very soul. The trust implicit in that sharing touched Susannah profoundly and filled her heart so full of love for him at times it felt as though it would surely burst.

Susannah had never been happier. In the three weeks since their return from Zach's Corners, every aspect of her life seemed to have taken an upswing.

A long talk with Marianne had cleared up any lingering hurt on both sides, and she and her sister-in-law were on their way to becoming the best of friends. Seth, who was proving to be a terrific nephew, had been delighted to discover that Susannah was his aunt. The alterations and repairs Jake ordered on the house were going well, and Susannah was registered for college and excited about going.

Life was so good it was almost scary. She didn't think it could possibly get better, but the news she received from Dr. Caldwell proved her wrong.

Pregnant. Susannah floated out of the doctor's office repeating the word over and over in her mind and grinning like a fool. By the time she reached her car, her hazy euphoria had given way to excitement, and she made a beeline for Jake's office.

Alice took one look at her and raised an elegant eyebrow. "Well, well. Expecting, are you?"

"How did you know?" Susannah squeaked.

"Sweetie, you're glowing like a neon sign. Have you told Jake?"

"Not yet. I just found out for certain myself." Susannah glanced at his office door. "Is he busy?"

"You know he's never too busy for you. Go on in."

Jake glanced up when she slipped inside his office. "Well, hello. This is a surprise." Tossing his pen aside, he rose and came around the desk.

The fluttery feeling in her stomach increased under his hot stare. When Susannah reached him, she went into his arms eagerly, and clung to him for support as she raised her head for his kiss.

The embrace was long and satisfying, but when it ended Jake frowned. "What's wrong? You're shaking."

"Nothing's wrong," Susannah said, giving him a sparkling look. "I'm just excited." Trying to act nonchalant, she smiled mysteriously and straightened his tie, and gave his lapel a wifely pat for good measure. Then she spoiled the whole effect by blurting out, "Oh, Jake, I have the most exciting news!"

"Oh? And what's th—"

The intercom buzzed, cutting him off. Jake grimaced and leaned over and pushed the button. "Yes, Alice, what is it?"

"There are two men out here, a Mr. Nathan Dushay and Mr. Philip Dushay, who insisted on seeing the C.E.O."

Startled, Susannah looked at Jake, her eyes widening. "My father and brother? What are they doing here?"

Jake's eyes narrowed. "Let's see, why don't we?" he murmured, and pressed the intercom button again. "Send them in, Alice."

A scant three seconds had lapsed when the door was thrust open and Nathan and Philip came striding in. A few feet inside they both jerked to a stop. "Good God! It *is* you!" Nathan said in an appalled voice. "When I saw that J. E. Taggart on the door, I thought it was just a nasty coincidence."

Standing motionless behind his desk, Jake looked at them across the wide expanse of polished mahogany. "As you can see, Dushay, I didn't marry your daughter to get my hands on your money. I don't need it. I own this company, and as of recently, several others, as well."

"That's why we're here, as you well know. Damn you, Taggart, you've got to stop."

"Stop? I'm just getting started."

"Jake, what's going on? What is he talking about?"

Nathan's enraged glare switched to his daughter. "This man you married is trying to ruin me, that's what I'm talking about."

"When we began to lose one after another of our sawmill customers, we knew there was a skunk in the woodpile, and we did some checking," Philip inserted angrily. "We discovered that a company by the name of Jetco was buying up the firms that made up our customer list, then canceling their contracts with the sawmill. Orders are so low we're operating in the red."

"Jake, is this true?"

"Yes," he replied with hard satisfaction.

"We came over here hoping to have a civilized meeting with Jetco's president and find out why they had targeted us, and what it would take to get the contracts back," Nathan said tightly, still addressing Susannah.

"Save your breath, Dushay. Before I'm through, you won't have any orders at all. I'm going to shut you down."

Susannah felt sick. She looked at Jake's cold face and wanted to weep. What a naive fool she'd been. Since their return from Zach's Corners, Jake had not mentioned the past or her family, and she'd thought he'd dropped his plans for revenge. She should have known better. "Jake, you can't close down the sawmill," she pleaded softly. "You must stop."

The look of astonished fury in his eyes almost made her cringe. "I don't believe this! You're trying to protect them, after they treated you like dirt?"

"You'll find, Taggart, that breeding will tell," Nathan sneered. "Our kind stick together."

"Oh, keep quiet, Father! This has nothing to do with you and Philip!" It was the first time in her life that Susannah had ever snapped back at her father, and he was so astonished he stared at her, slack-jawed.

She ignored him and turned to her husband, her expression pleading. "Jake, please. If you close down the mill it won't be just my father and Philip you'll be hurting. Think of all the people who depend on the mill for a living. The town's whole economy revolves around the sawmill."

Jake's face hardened. "You want me to protect the town? Save the jobs of all those 'good folks' in Zach's Corners who looked down their noses at the Taggarts for years? Why the hell should I?"

"Because they're not to blame in all this. Some of them may be prejudiced and petty, even downright mean, but most are just ordinary, hardworking people trying to get by. Don't punish them for my father's and Philip's sins, darling. Please. I beg you."

Nathan and Philip exchanged a tense look and watched Jake in silence waiting for his reply.

Susannah saw the fury and frustration in his eyes, the rigid way he held himself, and she knew a battle raged within him.

"For Pete's sake, Susannah," he ground out. "Breaking them financially is the only option I have left, and now you ask me to back off from that? I can't. Don't you understand? I can't."

"You must, my darling. Our whole future depends on it."

He looked at her sharply. "What are you saying?"

"That I can't stay with a man who would wantonly destroy the lives of innocent people," she replied sadly, her eyes beseeching him. "You have to choose which means the most to you, Jake—what we have together, or getting revenge on my father and brother. You can't have both."

For the briefest instant desperation flared in his eyes...then it was gone. As surely as if they were steel bars clanging into place, Susannah saw his defenses come up, saw him retreat behind that expressionless mask he hadn't used in her presence in weeks, and she felt cold inside.

"Be careful, sweetheart," he warned softly. "I don't take well to ultimatums."

"I'm sorry. You've left me with no other choice." She drew in a shuddering breath and blinked back tears. "When you know what it is you really want—" her voice broke, and she had to stop and press her quivering lips together for a moment before she could go on "—l-let me know. I'll be at home."

Susannah stood beside the balcony doors and stared out at the pewter sky. The day had begun with sunshine, but the weather had turned murky and threatening, and it seemed depressingly appropriate to her. After all, in the space of a few minutes her life had gone from glorious ecstasy to the depths of despair.

Where was Jake? It had been hours since she'd left his office. Susannah closed her eyes. *You have to trust him to make the right choice. If he loves you, he will.* She sighed. With every fiber in her being, she hoped that Marta was right.

The front door opened, and Susannah jumped. Shaking inside, she turned and waited.

Jake appeared in the doorway, his gaze zeroing in on her at once. Across the width of the elegant room, they looked at one another in silence. Finally he tossed his suit coat and briefcase on the sofa and crossed to where she stood, his face somber. Susannah's heart thumped wildly.

"The sawmill stays open," he said at last, and she went weak with relief.

"Oh, Jake, darling." Stepping forward, she slumped against him, her arms going around his waist. "I knew you'd do the right thing," she said tearfully against his chest. "I knew it."

Holding her close, he rocked her gently and laid his cheek against the top of her head. "Maybe you'd better reserve judgment until you hear what I've done."

She leaned back in his arms and looked at him warily. "You did reinstate the contracts so that Father could keep the sawmill open, didn't you?"

"Yes and no. I gave back the contracts, but I couldn't stomach doing business with Nathan. So I bought the sawmill. Plus all his other holdings in Zach's Corners. And before you ask, I gave him what the fair market value had been before I pulled the rug out from under him."

"Oh, Jake." Susannah smiled up at him lovingly, her heart so full it hurt. "You do realize, don't you, that you've gotten your revenge after all?"

"How do you figure?"

"The thing Father values most in life is being top dog. He'll never be able to stay in Zach's Corners now that all of his power is gone. You've run him out of town just as surely as he did the Taggarts."

Jake's eyes brightened at the thought, but only momentarily. "It's funny how things take on a new importance when you put them in perspective." He cupped her face in one hand and looked at her with such love that tears came to Susannah's eyes. "When I compared it to losing you, getting even with Nathan and Philip didn't seem important at all," he said deeply, and lowered his mouth to hers.

The kiss was so unbearably beautiful that Susannah came apart inside. She clung to him, trembling, tears streaming down her cheeks, her chest filled with a sweet ache. It was a kiss of healing for both of them, a balm for the pains of the past and a pledge of love unbroken for the future.

When at last it ended, Susannah tucked her head back against his chest and they held each other close, savoring the moment. Gazing dreamily out the balcony doors, she saw the setting sun peeking through the clouds, and she smiled.

"Jake?"

"Hmm?"

"Remember that exciting news I was going to tell you?"

"You mean before we were so rudely interrupted? Sure. What was it? Did the decorator find that wallpaper you wanted?"

"Even better than that." She drew in a deep breath. "I'm pregnant."

He grasped her shoulders and held her away from him. "A baby? You're going to have a baby?"

From his shocked expression it was impossible to tell whether he was happy or furious. Suddenly uneasy, Susannah bit her lower lip and nodded.

The next instant he surprised her by sweeping her up in his arms. "Jake! Where are you taking me?"

Ignoring her question, he carried her to their bedroom and laid her down on the bed as though she were made of glass, then he knelt beside it. She was about to protest that she wasn't an invalid but the words died on her lips when she saw his expression.

His hard face wore a look of absolute reverence. Slowly, as though he were touching something infinitely fragile and precious, he placed his splayed hand on her abdomen. The gesture was so exquisite that Susannah moaned. Then his vivid gaze sought hers, and the look in his eyes undid her completely. "I love you, Susannah," he whispered. The warmth of his hand was removed, and he bent and laid his cheek where his palm had been only a second before. "I love you."

MORE ABOUT
THE SCORPIO MAN

by Lydia Lee

All it took was one look into his piercing eyes and you knew you'd met your match: it was almost as if he had ESP and could read your every thought. And that wasn't all those dark eyes did. You were the first to look away, but when you glanced back up, he'd moved in on you. That's when you felt the heat, body heat, then pow! You don't actually remember what you talked about, though you did learn he was a Scorpio. *Scorpio!* Even people who don't believe in astrology tend to raise an eyebrow when someone confesses to being a Scorpion. Think *Richard Burton;* think *passion!* Ah, but that's just for starters.

So once you managed to pry yourself away from your Scorpio, you beat a hasty path to your local library and boned up on this legendary sign of the zodiac. Yep, there was that word again: *passion*. The kind that permeates everything the man does: his work, politics, religion and, yes, the woman—or women—in his life. He doesn't know what halfway measures are. It's all or nothing, and given his penchant for winning, it better be all. And if it's you he's after, nothing—not even a natural disaster—will stand in his way. Your Pluto-ruled man burns with a white heat, though being highly disciplined, he can cover his intensity with a cool facade. Don't be fooled; a bubbling cauldron lurks just beneath the surface. Let me stress right away, this is not a relationship to be taken lightly. You could get burned quite badly. Remember, playing with a Scorpio is tantamount to playing with fire. He won't tolerate other men in your life, and though he might not ask too many questions, if he suspects you of infidelity, he's capable of lashing out with that deadly tail of his. If he should appear to forgive you for any transgressions, be forewarned: he'll never forget.

Phew! Did I just write that to scare you? Not exactly. It's simply that every rose has its thorns—not that Scorpio is a rose, but he does have a magnificence and heroism about him that puts him head and shoulders above the crowd. His emotions run deep, so does his intellect, and once fully engaged, he'll scale any mountain, no matter how high, overcome any adversity and triumph in the end. He's both the archetypal hero *and* villain. His symbol encompasses a trinity: the deadly scorpion, who can sting his enemies or himself to death; the soaring eagle, who knows no fear; and the peaceful dove, who transcends all worldly concerns. Even though some Scorpios sort of slither between the heroic eagle and the deadly scorpion, never fully coming to grips with their true power, it is always within their capacity to rise from the murk and soar with the angels.

So where does your Scorpio stand—or soar, as the case may be? Well, if he shares that universal Scorpionic trait of secrecy, it may take a while for you to figure out. Ah, you see, this man will not reveal himself all at once. In fact, it may just take a lifetime together. He, on the other hand, will take delight in quickly psyching you out, for nothing so intrigues him as a mystery. Perhaps that's why Scorpios make such excellent detectives and psychiatrists. And if you remember your first eye contact with him, you'll probably want to add hypnotist to his career possibilities.

So, if you're made of sturdy material and are ready for an adventure that will last a lifetime, Scorpio might just be for you. For beneath that cool, calm exterior, you'll find not only his legendary passion and prowess, but a surprising tenderness and loyalty, and a warmth that will take the chill off even the frostiest of evenings. For this is a man you can not only soar with, but one who will bring you safely back down to earth.

* * * * *

FAMOUS SCORPIO MEN

Richard Burton
Pablo Picasso
Burt Lancaster
Carl Sagan
Jonas Salk

COMING NEXT MONTH

#832 ARC OF THE ARROW—Rita Rainville
Written in the Stars
Brandy Cochran thought accountants were quiet and dull—but no one could accuse R. G. Travers of being boring! The sexy Sagittarian's determined pursuit made her nervous . . . but so did the idea of life without him. . . .

#833 THE COWBOY AND THE CHAUFFEUR—Elizabeth August
Rachel Hadley hadn't expected much from life, but rugged cowboy Logan James was determined to change that. He swept the cool chauffeur out of the driver's seat and into the arms of love—his arms!

#834 SYDNEY'S FOLLY—Kasey Michaels
Sydney Blackmun's latest "project" was getting the oh-so-serious Blake Mansfield involved in Ocean City's surfside fun. But could she convince her new neighbor that their love was more than a summer folly?

#835 MISTLETOE AND MIRACLES—Linda Varner
Being trapped with playboy author Matt Foxx was *not* efficiency expert Kirby Gibson's idea of a merry Christmas. Matt broke every rule she had, but how could Kirby resist a man who kissed so well?

#836 DONE TO PERFECTION—Stella Bagwell
Caterer Julia Warren knew how she'd like to serve all lawyers—well-done! But Judge Harris Hargrove was determined to prove that he was to Julia's taste. . . .

#837 TOO GOOD TO BE TRUE—Victoria Glenn
Ashli Wilkerson didn't know why she was upset that real-estate developer Kyle Hamilton was engaged to her sister—she didn't even *like* the man! But liking had little to do with loving. . . .

AVAILABLE THIS MONTH:

#826 STING OF THE SCORPION
Ginna Gray

#827 LOVE SHY
Marcine Smith

#828 SHERMAN'S SURRENDER
Pat Tracy

#829 FOR BRIAN'S SAKE
Patti Standard

#830 GOLD DIGGER
Arlene James

#831 LADY IN DISTRESS
Brittany Young

Take 4 bestselling love stories FREE

Plus get a FREE surprise gift!

SILHOUETTE®
OFFICIAL SWEEPSTAKES
RULES

NO PURCHASE NECESSARY

1. To enter, complete an Official Entry Form or 3"× 5" index card by hand-printing, in plain block letters, your complete name, address, phone number and age, and mailing it to: Silhouette Fashion A Whole New You Sweepstakes, P.O. Box 9056, Buffalo, NY 14269-9056.

   No responsibility is assumed for lost, late or misdirected mail. Entries must be sent separately with first class postage affixed, and be received no later than December 31, 1991 for eligibility.

2. Winners will be selected by D.L. Blair, Inc., an independent judging organization whose decisions are final, in random drawings to be held on January 30, 1992 in Blair, NE at 10:00 a.m. from among all eligible entries received.

3. The prizes to be awarded and their approximate retail values are as follows: Grand Prize — A brand-new Ford Explorer 4×4 plus a trip for two (2) to Hawaii, including round-trip air transportation, six (6) nights hotel accommodation, a $1,400 meal/spending money stipend and $2,000 cash toward a new fashion wardrobe (approximate value: $28,000) or $15,000 cash; two (2) Second Prizes — A trip to Hawaii, including round-trip air transportation, six (6) nights hotel accommodation, a $1,400 meal/spending money stipend and $2,000 cash toward a new fashion wardrobe (approximate value: $11,000) or $5,000 cash; three (3) Third Prizes — $2,000 cash toward a new fashion wardrobe. All prizes are valued in U.S. currency. Travel award air transportation is from the commercial airport nearest winner's home. Travel is subject to space and accommodation availability, and must be completed by June 30, 1993. Sweepstakes offer is open to residents of the U.S. and Canada who are 21 years of age or older as of December 31, 1991, except residents of Puerto Rico, employees and immediate family members of Torstar Corp., its affiliates, subsidiaries, and all agencies, entities and persons connected with the use, marketing, or conduct of this sweepstakes. All federal, state, provincial, municipal and local laws apply. Offer void wherever prohibited by law. Taxes and/or duties, applicable registration and licensing fees, are the sole responsibility of the winners. Any litigation within the province of Quebec respecting the conduct and awarding of a prize may be submitted to the Régie des loteries et courses du Québec. All prizes will be awarded; winners will be notified by mail. No substitution of prizes is permitted.

4. Potential winners must sign and return any required Affidavit of Eligibility/Release of Liability within 30 days of notification. In the event of noncompliance within this time period, the prize may be awarded to an alternate winner. Any prize or prize notification returned as undeliverable may result in the awarding of that prize to an alternate winner. By acceptance of their prize, winners consent to use of their names, photographs or their likenesses for purposes of advertising, trade and promotion on behalf of Torstar Corp. without further compensation. Canadian winners must correctly answer a time-limited arithmetical question in order to be awarded a prize.

5. For a list of winners (available after 3/31/92), send a separate stamped, self-addressed envelope to: Silhouette Fashion A Whole New You Sweepstakes, P.O. Box 4665, Blair, NE 68009.

PREMIUM OFFER TERMS

To receive your gift, complete the Offer Certificate according to directions. Be certain to enclose the required number of "Fashion A Whole New You" proofs of product purchase (which are found on the last page of every specially marked "Fashion A Whole New You" Silhouette or Harlequin romance novel). Requests must be received no later than December 31, 1991. Limit: four (4) gifts per name, family, group, organization or address. Items depicted are for illustrative purposes only and may not be exactly as shown. Please allow 6 to 8 weeks for receipt of order. Offer good while quantities of gifts last. In the event an ordered gift is no longer available, you will receive a free, previously unpublished Silhouette or Harlequin book for every proof of purchase you have submitted with your request, plus a refund of the postage and handling charge you have included. Offer good in the U.S. and Canada only.

SLFW - SWPR

SILHOUETTE® OFFICIAL SWEEPSTAKES ENTRY FORM

4-FWSRS-4

Complete and return this Entry Form immediately – the more entries you submit, the better your chances of winning!

- Entries must be received by **December 31, 1991.**
- A Random draw will take place on **January 30, 1992.**
- No purchase necessary.

Yes, I want to win a FASHION A WHOLE NEW YOU Sensuous and Adventurous prize from Silhouette:

Name _____ Telephone _____ Age _____

Address _____

City _____ State _____ Zip _____

Return Entries to: **Silhouette FASHION A WHOLE NEW YOU,**
P.O. Box 9056, Buffalo, NY 14269-9056   © 1991 Harlequin Enterprises Limited

PREMIUM OFFER

To receive your free gift, send us the required number of proofs-of-purchase from any specially marked FASHION A WHOLE NEW YOU Silhouette or Harlequin Book with the Offer Certificate properly completed, plus a check or money order (do not send cash) to cover postage and handling payable to Silhouette FASHION A WHOLE NEW YOU Offer. We will send you the specified gift.

OFFER CERTIFICATE

Item	A. SENSUAL DESIGNER VANITY BOX COLLECTION (set of 4) (Suggested Retail Price $60.00)	B. ADVENTUROUS TRAVEL COSMETIC CASE SET (set of 3) (Suggested Retail Price $25.00)
# of proofs-of-purchase	18	12
Postage and Handling	$3.50	$2.95
Check one	☐	☐

Name _____

Address _____

City _____ State _____ Zip _____

Mail this certificate, designated number of proofs-of-purchase and check or money order for postage and handling to: **Silhouette FASHION A WHOLE NEW YOU Gift Offer,** P.O. Box 9057, Buffalo, NY 14269-9057. Requests must be received by December 31, 1991.

ONE PROOF-OF-PURCHASE

4-FWSRP-4

To collect your fabulous free gift you must include the necessary number of proofs-of-purchase with a properly completed Offer Certificate.

© 1991 Harlequin Enterprises Limited

See previous page for details.